TO
LAUGH
FOR

Desmond Shepherd

Started writing (in my head only): Early February 2024

Started writing (actual words on a computer screen): February 27, 2024

Completed First Draft (consists of writing the entire book and brief once-through proofread of each chapter): April 25, 2024

First Draft Word Count: 50,354

Completed Final Manuscript: May 6, 2024

Final Manuscript Word Count: 50,524

Time spent writing, editing, proofreading, designing cover, formatting book, marketing, reformatting book, fixing more typos, walking away multiple times, and saying "I'm done with this!": Immeasurable.

1

"WELL, HMM. I suppose … I suppose to get to the other side?"

Jerry Stinson wasn't sure why he said it. There was kind of this crack. A little pop in his brain. A flutter in his abdomen. Something that caused the corners of his mouth to form a closed parenthesis fallen on its side.

His brain said, "I stop accepting this form of life. We must forge a new path."

And, well, it did forge a new path.

Because the current path for Jerry had become this drudgery through mud, flicking the shoes and socks off each night and slipping on a clean pair the following day.

Here. Let's put this in perspective. Let's run through a day in the life of Jerry Stinson. Though we'll focus on today because today is when things changed.

6:00 AM. The alarm clock vibrates and squeals. Now, Jerry doesn't need an alarm clock. He's already lying flat on his back, eyes staring at the ceiling. He waits for it. Counts the seconds in his head until it hits 6:00 AM. Sometimes, his guess and count are on the money. Most times, he's nowhere near it.

Internal clock aside, he slaps a hand on the top of the clock. Shuts it up. Gives it another nine minutes to come roaring back. He counts again. Hopes he'll get a little closer this time.

He's delaying the inevitable.

A day like every other day.

An existence of evenness.

The status quo.

"Eight minutes, thirty-seven seconds. Eight minutes, forty—"

The alarm rings, and this time, his hand slaps the off button. Torso rotates 90 degrees. Feet plop to the floor. And he sits there.

Just sits there.

Downstairs, a few bangs work their way from the kitchen and up the hallway. Bam. Bam. Bam. Cabinets opening, closing.

Different day. Same routine.

Jerry lets out a long sigh, places his hands on his knees with a smack, smack, smack, and moves to a standing position. Showers next. Shaves next. Hits every contour of the face and chin, careful with his butterfly razor, not a knick or scratch. Parts the sands of hair to the right. Back to the bedroom. Clothes on. Straight gray suit. Bright white button-up. Impossibly blue tie. Shoes that swallow the light around them like a black hole on his feet.

Down the stairs. To the kitchen.

There's Carl. Carl Calabrese. Round head. Round body. Jerry could nearly pick him up and roll him down a lane. Hit ten pins, and he'd have a strike.

"Morning, Carl," Jerry says.

"Morning, Jerry," Carl says.

"Sleep well."

"Did. Sure did. You?"

"Did."

Carl sits at the table. Bowl in front of him. Box next to the bowl. A half-gallon milk jug that's three-quarters gone next to that. A spoon grasped in his right hand shovels downward, brings up a scoop and a few drips back to the bowl, and then evacuates into his mouth. Mouth closes. Teeth crunch, food starting its trip through the human body.

"By the way," Carl says after finishing the bite, "I'll have my portion of the rent for you end of this week. Promise."

"Thank you," is all Jerry can say.

2

It's the same day. The same routine. Carl can't ever seem to put together the cash to pay his portion of the rent on time. He's in a perpetual state of debt, catching up on what he owes but always behind on the current bill.

And what can Jerry do? It's not like he'd kick Carl out because he didn't pay rent. He had more than enough money to cover both. But it's the principle.

The principle of the matter is that all people need to be responsible. And Jerry had no intention of letting any single rent payment slide. But still, he'd never let the frustration show. No matter how much it bothered him.

"Want some," Carl says as he grabs the box and tilts it toward Jerry. "Still a little left."

"I'm quite fine. The office will have croissants."

"Very well." The box taps back to the table.

"No coffee?" Jerry asks.

Every day, Carl made the coffee. Every. Single. Day.

And yet, the pot sits cold inside an unplugged machine. Jerry's brain snaps at him, thinks maybe he sees things wrong. He grabs the handle, lifts the pot to his left eye, and circles it on the circumference.

Not a drop. Not a single drop.

"Broken," Carl says. "Thing won't do a thing. Dead. It's dead."

Jerry breathes in deep through his nose. Back out. Lowers his heartbeat.

It'll be fine. Coffee is at the office, too. I'll be fine.

"Well, I best be getting to it then," Jerry says.

Carl gives a nod. Not a nod like he's got to get moving and out the door, too. Just a nod like "Have a good day. I'll be sitting here all day long doing nothing and *especially* not looking for a job."

Another slow breath in and out, and Jerry's out the door.

Drive down the road. Follow the signs. Follow the lights. Follow the lines. Turn right. Left. Straight. Straight some more.

Stop. Wait for the green left turn arrow. Turn left. Drive some more.

The last leg of the race to purgatory kind of melts off the back of Jerry's neck, and he now stands at the front door with block letters CAF (the abbreviation for where he works) on it. CAF stands for "Carson Accounting Firm", an accounting firm housing 50 or so employees on three or so stories of a ten or so story-high building.

Up the stairs, turn left. A bunch of heads tilted down toward computer monitors stay just like that. Keys click on keyboards. Each step forward, Jerry glances into a passed cubicle, but not a single pair of eyes turns his way.

But the thing is, he doesn't care. He doesn't need a greeting. A "Hello." A "Hey, how'd your night go?" A "Hey, you watch the game? Want to come over tonight to watch the next one?" None of that.

And yet, on this day, he passes a cubicle just three away from his, and his pace slows, his gaze lingers. There sits Jeanine Garrison. Like the others, her eyeballs glare at a screen with a spreadsheet of rows and columns, numbers, and profits and losses. Jerry's feet barely move. Nearly stop.

Until Jeanine's gaze shifts. Her head tilts upward, strands of blond hair fall back, revealing her face. Then, the rest of her body, which is adorned in a similar color and style as the very suit Jerry wears but modified for a female's more appealing design. Before her pupils land on his form, his feet shuffle a few steps quicker and onward to his cubicle. Plops his buttocks on the chair.

The next few hours consist of crunching numbers. Calling clients. Letting them know how they've made too much money and need to find a way to legally hide so much money so they don't have to pay a good portion of that money to the government. There might be a little more nuance to it than that, but at the end of the day, that's what every client wants: To keep the most amount of money they can and not give it away.

"Stinson," a voice calls four cubicles down and approaches fast.

Jerry jumps at the call, shaken a little by an adrenaline rush, and he's suddenly completely aware of the throbbing in his skull because he forgot to get himself a cup of coffee when he made it into the office. The grumble in his stomach isn't helping. How could he forget the croissants, too?

Pushing that to the side, he turns away from the monitor to see Bill Carson standing at his cubicle entrance. Carson is, for all intents and purposes, an annoying little nuisance. Son of the owner of CAF. Couldn't add two and two to save his life, but nepotism has its perks, so Jerry answered to Carson.

"Yes, sir," Jerry said.

"Where's the Bluth report? I needed it yesterday." Carson stands there, arms straight at his side, mustache trimmed like someone drew a line above his lip with a pen.

"The Bluth report?" Jerry questions, using the moment to formulate his thoughts and access the part of his mind that recalls the Bluth report.

"Yes, the Bluth report. I'm supposed to meet with the client in 15 minutes, Jerry. Fifteen minutes. And I got nothing."

Enough time passes for Jerry's brain to reveal what happened with the Bluth report. With all the numbers and crunching and reporting that Jerry does, remembering all the details of what he's completed and yet to be done blurs some.

"Well, sir, on Monday, I—"

"Get to the point, Stinson!"

"I gave it to you Monday."

"Monday?"

"Yes, walked into your office with the manila folder. Papers in hand. You weren't there. I set it on top of your desk. Next to a cup of coffee." But was it a cup of coffee, or was Jerry's brain trying to remind him of something? "And a stack of other folders."

"Next to or on top?"

"Next to."

"Well, I got news for you, Stinson, the report isn't there. I searched my office thoroughly. You think I want to come all this way to your cubicle to ask you about it? Waste my time?"

This is when Jerry first felt the tickle. That something in his brain that told him to say a few unexpected words despite the seriousness of the situation. He couldn't quite find the words, but they were there. His tongue was a diving board, and the diver was about to jump off.

"I'm sorry, sir. I should have made sure to hand it to you directly."

"You better believe you should have. Better believe."

"I could email it to you. I have the report right here on my computer."

"Email? You know my requirements. Paper, Jerry, paper. Nothing good ever came from a computer but bugs and glitches and stolen information. *If I had it my way*, I'd remove all the computers." And now Carson's voice carries to every wall, "All of them from every single one of your desks."

Jerry imagines heads lifting. Eyes turning cubicle corners. His mouth also makes to form a word his brain says is the first in a sentence that would bring him great pleasure. Such an odd sensation. One he's never felt before, nor one he gathers he could explain. But before the word begins to start the phrase that makes a sentence—

"No, Jerry. No! This is incompetence. This is an unwillingness to follow procedure."

So, this isn't a typical day for Jerry. Because a typical day would have him doing his work. Punching the keys. Punching the clock. Exiting the building and returning home. Dinner. Brush teeth. Remove contacts. Pajamas. Sleep. Do it all again tomorrow. But today, that's not what happens.

Today, it all changes.

"Maybe I oughta make an example of you." Carson's eyes scan the room. The son of the owner of CAF. The guy underneath the head honcho. The one everyone wishes to ignore but must pay attention to. "Yeah, an example. That's what we need to instill the right kind of fear and dedication.

"Jerry Stinson," Carson says, eyes like bullets. "You're fired!"

Fired? "Fired, sir?"

"Yeah. Pack up your stuff. Get out of here. Find someone else who's willing to tolerate the insubordination."

"Insubordination?"

This confuses Jerry to no end. He always knew Carson was a chore to work for but had never expected something like this. It came without warning, barely with cause. But it was the truth. Words stated, facts presented.

"Yes, in..sub..ord..ination."

Jerry's brain. Oh, Jerry's brain. It conjures some things up. Some great things to say. The words jumble into all kinds of mixed bags of goodies.

No. I couldn't. I wouldn't. And why would I even say them? They are so unexpected. But obvious. And maybe even contradictory. I can't.

Jerry stands, dazed. Sucker-punched. The moment sinks in, but even still, he hopes the boat will float. All the things that happen now. Bills to pay. Rent to cover. It's not like Carl will come to the rescue. He scans the room. Tops of heads peer over the cubicle walls. Eyes angle at their respective viewpoints to see a man instantly emasculated.

"Very well, sir," is all Jerry can say. All he can conjure his mouth and vocal cords to spew when his brain wants him to say so much more.

Turning to his desk, he fishes an empty box from underneath. Gathers his belongings: A picture frame with the stock photo. A pen he one time brought in from home. And a coffee mug that says

"World's Best Dad" was there from the guy who worked at the desk before him. So, okay, maybe not all his belongings. But he'd drank enough coffee from that mug to have squatter's rights.

Box in hand, he marches back the way he entered. Past the coffee and croissants. Past heads that ignored his arrival but gaze in awe as he departs. Even Jeanine. She stands there. A frown that wrinkles the corners of her mouth, eyes lowered in pity.

"I'm sorry, Jerry," she whispers.

She knows my name? I never imagined.

"It'll be fine," he says. "Fine."

But will it be fine? This is nothing like the life he's led to this point. A life of evenness. The status quo. Day in, day out. Maybe he can find another job. As an accountant. Crunching numbers. Eying spreadsheets. But is that what he wants?

His brain tells him something otherwise. It fizzles and pops like a shaken can of soda. It wants him to say things about this situation. Not keep it bottled up with the cap on. No, his brain tells him it's time for a change. But he punches it in the left eye. Tells it to shut up.

He reaches the exit to the maze of cubicles and turns toward his colleagues. They all stare. Just stare like he's a deer hit by a semi-trailer truck, flailing in agony before the last breath and spasm leaves his existence.

Carson stands at the other end. A superhero with fists on his hips. His lips spread board straight, brows furrowed. Triumphant in the face of "insubordination".

Jerry turns away. Down the stairs. Turns right. Makes his way out of CAF, never to return. The street bustles with moving cars, the sidewalk with pedestrians. Where should he go? His car? He's not sure. He's a man holding a box with three things in it. He doesn't know which direction to take.

On any other day, he'd get in his car. Drive away. Drive some more. Turn right. Straight. Go straight some more. Right. Turn left.

Follow the lines. Follow the lights. Follow the signs. Drive up the road.

And he's home.

But today isn't a typical end-of-the-work-day kind of day. It's an end-of-work-period kind of day. So he tries something a little different. Box held at his chest, he serpentines the sea of people crossing his path. Feet take him a block away from CAF. Another part of town. Another life. Still full of the same bustle of people with jobs. Or maybe not. Maybe they're aimlessly roaming the city, too, because they have nowhere else to be. A bunch of Carl Calabreses with no purpose in life.

He finally settles down, legs aching, body weary of the twists and turns to avoid people and keep hold of his box. He's at a corner. Street lights on each side. Opposite the street, a palmed hand lighted in red tells him to stay put so he doesn't walk over the crosswalk, and a vehicle splats him to the ground in a mix of colorful bodily fluids.

And then he stands there. He just stands there. Wonders what he's going to do. So lost in thought, he jumps when a voice next to his right ear says, "What's in the box?"

Jerry's gaze turns to a pencil of a man. Towers over him by at least a third of his height. The man peers over into the box.

"World's greatest dad, huh?" the pencil man says. "How many kids do you have?"

"Oh, I don't have kids. No kids at all."

"Just yourself."

"Just me … well, and Carl."

"Who's Carl?"

"My roommate."

"He get you the mug?"

"No."

"Wouldn't have thought so, especially since you don't have kids."

"Very true. True."

Cars whiz by. The red hand still says to stay put and not cross the street.

"I take this path every day," the man says. "Light won't change for at least two minutes. Longest light in town."

"Is it?"

"Is."

While all the cars move at full speed, a truck passes in front of Jerry and the man. Its back end is slotted, and through the holes, layers of shelves hold a variety of chickens. Painted on the side of the truck is a white chicken giving a thumbs-up with one of its feathered wings, so really, a feather up, and below that, it says "Chicken House Foods".

The truck comes to a stop just beyond them and at the curb. Both Jerry and the man watch the truck, eyes fixated as a single chicken head pokes through one of the slots. The head wriggles and writhes, moving nearly 180 degrees. The neck pokes through now. And next, a wing. The hen clucks some, twists and turns, and the other wing protrudes from the slot. Now, half the chicken hangs from the truck.

The truck's muffler spits out some black smoke and jerks forward. The movement gives the hen a little push, causing the rest of its body to slide through the opening. It lands on the road, wings flapping a dropping flight.

And then it stands there. Bobs its head a few times. Turns and hops onto the sidewalk. In that haphazard way that chickens do, it weaves around the people on the path. Most jump out of its way. Some point. Quite rapidly, the hen runs right up to Jerry and the man, wings fluttering a few times until it stops next to the man. Faces the red palm across the street.

Neither Jerry nor the man says anything to the chicken. In fact, they even turn their heads away from it. All vehicles traveling come to a screeching halt in front of them. A horn or two honks. The red palm goes black, and a white stick figure of a man walking illuminates. Jerry is about to step on the crosswalk when the hen suddenly moves forward.

Both Jerry and the man stand there and watch as the hen goes straight across the crosswalk, in front of all the cars, until it reaches the opposite area. It turns left and out of sight, bobbing its head and weaving unpredictably through the crowd.

The white-lighted stick figure flashes. But still, Jerry and the man can't bring their feet to move them along. The chicken's apparent appreciation for the law of the road and to not jaywalk dumbfounds them to immobility.

The red palm shines again, and traffic zips along with squeals and a horn honk or two.

"Now," the man says, eyes fixed on the last location of the hen, "what do you ... why do you think that chicken crossed the road?"

And this is where we fall in line with the outset. Here is where Jerry decided to give in to the crack. The little pop in his brain. The flutter in his abdomen. That something that caused the corners of his mouth to form a closed parenthesis fallen on its side. Its right side to be specific and avoid confusion.

"Well, hmm. I suppose ... I suppose to get to the other side?"

And with the words, a large smile formed on Jerry's face. He felt good. Happy. Euphoric. Elated. Even despite losing his job. It was such a satisfying statement in the form of a question. A completely obvious observation but yet nothing near what any one person would be expected to say.

But also, the words impacted the pencil of a man. Because as much as Jerry thought the words were unexpected, he knew he would say them. The man had no idea they were coming.

They hit him like a *Chicken House Foods* truck.

First, the man's abdomen moved in and out like a hiccup. He blurted a grunt from his vocal cords. Then, a gasp of air. Then, a pushing out of air. This repeated, louder. His body shook with an increased intensity. The sounds from his voice box turned up the volume knob a little more. The shaking more rapid. He bent over, hands on his knees, vocal and vibrating. Then he collapsed to the ground, on his side, holding his abdomen. No longer was the sound coming from his mouth, but his head and lips moved as if they should be. No air passed through, in and out. Just silence, an open mouth, teeth exposed, jaw undulating.

"Hey," Jerry said. "Hey, are you alright?"

But the pencil man said nothing. Just continued his action, as if something controlled his body and forced him to be subservient. The man's eyeballs bulged even as the smile on his face widened.

People on the street now stopped. Watched a man shaking on the ground. Some gathered around, bewildered looks on their faces. "What's wrong with him?" "What happened?" "Is he okay?"

And then the man stopped. Not just the shaking, not just the movement. But stopped completely. No motion. No words. Stared straight ahead with an open smile. Pure joy frozen in time.

"Does he have a pulse?" someone yelled.

Jerry scanned the crowd for the unknown speaker. It was hard to tell who said it. All eyes stared at the man, some at Jerry. All willed Jerry to check on the man because he stood inches from him.

Box still in hand, Jerry bent down. Set it on the concrete, careful not to allow the mug to rattle around inside and crack. Now to his knees, he reached his index and middle fingers to the man's neck. Touched the skin, still warm. Searched for the heartbeat. Repositioned. Searched again. Farther up. Search. Down. Search. Right. Search. Left. Search.

Nothing. "Nothing," Jerry whispered.

"What's that?"

Jerry turned to the crowd, eyes all waiting for him to announce his verdict. Fingers still on the man's neck.

"I think ... I think... Well, I'm no doctor. I'm just an

accountant. *Was* an accountant. But I think he's dead."

"Oh no!" "Call emergency services!" "Life's too short!" "Don't look, honey." "Crazy!"

Jerry stood as the crowd gathered closer. He backed away from the man, into the sea of people. Mixed into them like someone pouring milk into the batter of a cake.

He ran to his car. Drove away. Drove some more. Turned right. Straight. Went straight some more. Right. Turned left. Followed the lines. Followed the lights. Followed the signs. Drove up the road.

And he was home and wasn't one hundred percent positive, but he was pretty sure he had just killed a pencil of a man.

2

JERRY LAID IN bed staring up at the ceiling. But it's not 6:00 AM. He wasn't counting the seconds until his alarm clock buzzed. No. It was 8:00 PM or thereabouts, by Jerry's estimation, since he hadn't checked the clock in what he guessed was about an hour.

"To get to the other side."

Could it be? Could words hold such impact so as to kill a man? It's all he could imagine. All his brain could deduce based on the progression of events that unfolded before his eyes.

And the way things transpired once he got home did little to convince him that the words can't kill, despite what others told him.

Here. This is what happened when Jerry arrived home.

Jerry walks in the door. His hand shakes. Lips tremble.

To the kitchen. He hasn't eaten all day. That'll do it. That'll calm him down. The box of cereal sits in the spot where Carl placed it. Just a box. Nearly empty. He pries it open, examines the inside. Thinks about a bowl. Thinks about a spoon. Thinks about the quarter of a half-gallon of milk sitting on the table from the morning because Carl was too lazy to put it away.

He opts to avoid sour milk.

Forgets the spoon.

Uses the tools God gave him and plunges his hand into the box. Pulls out a handful. Stuffs it in his mouth. Chomps. Chomps.

"Jerry, you're home?" Carl says, entering the kitchen.

"I am, Carl. Am." There it is again. A remark his brain wants him to make that's quite obvious and would bring him joy. But he suppresses it. It's not like Carl and him are best friends. But he doesn't want to see him dead either.

Carl steps to the table. Takes a chair. Sits on it. Leans back. Hands support his head.

"Why are you home so soon?" Carl asks.

"It's a long story," Jerry says. "Very long. But I suppose I have the time. Something happened today. Something I can't quite explain."

Jerry slams another hand in the box. Pulls out some marshmallows that he imagines are sugar-coated Styrofoam. Pops them in his mouth. Not bad. But not good either.

"What happened?" Carl asks.

"Well, let me tell you." Jerry sits across from Carl. Wishes the coffeemaker worked. "I was standing on the sidewalk. Waiting to cross the street. This man's next to me. Asks me if you bought me the 'World's Best Dad' mug when—"

"Why'd he think I bought it? You don't even have kids."

"I know."

"And why do you have a mug that says that?"

"I inherited it."

"And how'd he know about me?"

"Because I told him after he asked if I had kids."

"Naturally."

"Naturally. So there's this chicken truck. Pulls past us. A chicken squeezes out. Comes and stands right next to us."

"Both of you at the same time? In between?"

"No, next to the man."

"So?"

"So then the light changes for us to cross. But we don't cross. The chicken... The chicken acts like it knows what it's doing. Follows the crosswalk in a straight path and makes it over before the lights change again."

"Weird."

"Yes. Very. Very odd."

"I wonder why the chicken crossed the road?"

"The man asked me the same thing."

"And what did you say?"

"Well, I said—"

Jerry stops himself. The tickle is there. His brain wants him to say it. But he knows he shouldn't. Say it, and Carl is dead. Kaput. Motionless. Xs for eyes.

"Nothing. I said nothing."

Carl's face twists. Eyes squint. "That can't be true. Can't be true at all. You seemed about ready to explode right now until you stopped yourself."

"Was not."

"Was."

"OK. Trust me, though. I can't tell you."

"Why not?"

"Because." Jerry tries to think of an excuse, a reason. *Because it's not your business. Not your concern. Quit meddling.* But none of that parts his lips. "Just because."

"Not good enough, Jerry. Not good enough at all." Carl taps the table with both his index fingers. Rat-a-tat-tat. "The man and I both asked the same question. And you have the same answer. Now tell me."

Jerry has had about enough of this. He won't say it, but he'd tell Carl the effect. "Fine. It was something so obvious and unexpected all at once. Words to surprise. Words that create some sort of ... of reaction. The human body is unable to withstand it. So I'm not telling what it was because if I did, the words might kill you."

"Kill me? Whoever heard of such a thing? Knives kill. Guns kill. And the people behind the knives and guns kill. But I've never heard any such thing as words that kill. You're building this up to be quite the statement. Or you're lying about the entire thing."

16

Jerry boils. Rapid bubbles pop all over his skull. Evaporate into steam. Rise skyward. Condensate and pour down. It's clear Carl isn't going to let this go.

With much reluctance, Jerry says, "You win. I'll tell you what I said. But I warned you."

"Naturally." Carl sits back in the chair, ready to take the brunt of the words. "Now you've built this up to be quite something. I have a hard time believing it can be as amazing and damaging as you claim."

Jerry considers this plight. Carl can be a pest. But he in no way deserves this any more than that pencil of man did. He almost feels sorry for Carl's insistence on knowing what was said … almost. He'd been warned.

"When the man asked me why the chicken crossed the road, I told him—" Jerry pauses, the fear of killing another man hitting him.

"Go ahead," Carl says.

Oh, fine! "I said—"

A rapid rapping on the front door swings Jerry's head and Carl's head toward the sound's direction. The action reveals to Jerry that if a sound could make a person move, then words might definitely be able to kill.

"You expecting someone?" Carl asks.

"No. You?" Jerry responds.

"Well if I were I wouldn't ask you if you were, so the answer is no."

The knock comes again. This time, a little louder. Just as rapid.

"Best to see who it is," Carl says with a nod, motioning toward the front door.

"Yes, best to."

Jerry pushes away from the table, grabs another handful of sugar-coated Styrofoam pieces, and stuffs them in his mouth. As his jaw works its magic on the morsels, he opens the doors to the sight of Jeanine Garrison.

"Jeanine," Jerry says through garbled words. "What are you doing here?"

"Jerry. Hello." Her head lowers, and she glances to the floor. "May I come in?"

Jerry performs a big swallow, nearly chokes on the pieces he chewed improperly. "Of course. Yes. Please." He steps aside, and Jeanine slips through the doorway. "I must say I'm a little perplexed. This morning, I didn't think you even knew who I was. Then I realized you knew my name. And now you're at my home."

"I'm sorry for showing up unannounced."

"Who is it?" Carl calls from the kitchen.

"Jeanine, from work," Jerry calls back. "Well, formerly my work."

"I don't know any, Jeanine," Carl calls. "And what do you mean 'formerly'?"

"Sorry, am I intruding?" Jeanine asks.

"No. Not at all," Jerry says. "Come in."

They walk to the kitchen where Carl sits, licking powdery sugar and crumbs from his hands. He puts his hand in the cereal box but comes up empty.

"Are you Jeanine?" Carl asks.

"Yes," Jeanine says.

"I'm Carl."

"Hi, Carl."

"Right," Jerry says. "Now that we know each other. Jeanine, are you thirsty?"

"No, why?"

"Because if you were, I'd offer you a drink. But since you aren't, please, have a seat. We can all talk."

Jeanine looks from Carl to Jerry. Back to Carl. Now Jerry.

"I'm sorry about what happened today," Jeanine finally says. "You know, losing your job and all."

"You lost your job!" Carl says. "This is quite the news. No wonder you were home early. Seems like you would've led with that instead of a story about a chicken."

"Oh, yes," Jeanine says. "The chicken."

"You know about the chicken?" Jerry asks.

"Have you started looking for another job?" Carl asks.

There's the boil again. Blood pressure rises. Cheeks warm. Teeth grit and clench. Carl has some nerve when he hadn't held any job for more than two weeks and goes months at a time without one.

"No," is all Jerry says. Just "No."

"Yes, I know about the chicken." Jeanine bites the bottom of her lip. "I have to confess, after Carson fired you, I felt so bad. He's such an annoying little nuisance."

"I say the same thing all the time."

"Really?"

"Yes. Well ... in my head, at least."

"So when are you going to start looking for another job?" Carl says.

"Well, soon, of course. It just happened."

"You didn't deserve it," Jeanine says. "You know, I'm the one who checks everyone's work. I'm the accountant's accountant. Your work is always impeccable. Accurate. To the point. It was unwarranted for him to fire you."

"Thank you."

"You're welcome."

"We have enough money for the rent?" Carl asks.

"I only got fired today, Carl. It's not like they took all the money I have in the bank, too." Turning to Jeanine. "So, you know about the chicken?"

"Yes. I figured I'd track you down. See if you were okay. Pretty much tell you what I told you right now. But you moved pretty fast. Up through the people. To the next block."

"I didn't know where I was going, weaving around like that.

Shock, I think. Shock."

"Well, hopefully, it doesn't take you too long to find another job," Carl says.

Whack. Bam. Kaboom. Jerry wants to slam his hand on the table. Rattle it. Vibrate the warm milk just to the edge causing it to fall and spill all over the floor in a curdled mess causing Jeanine and Carl to lift from their seats a split second and drop down.

But he doesn't do any of that.

"Right now, that's not important. Jeanine, I apologize for Carl. Now, please, tell me what you know about the chicken."

"It's quite alright," Jeanine says. "You're friend—

"He's not my friend."

"You're roommate, then, wasn't a bother."

What an interesting woman! Kind. Diplomatic. Thoughtful. A sum of things that went beyond Jerry's superficial attraction all those days he saw her at work but never spoke to or with her.

"But anyway," Jeanine continues, "you were standing at that corner. Holding that box. I was almost to you when the chicken truck pulled by. I saw this chicken pop out. Ran right over to you and some man. He was talking to you."

"Yes. And then what?"

"Well, I didn't want to interrupt the conversation. So I waited. Thought maybe he'd cross the street. Or maybe I should turn around and let you go about your business. Then the chicken crosses the road. You two don't move. I'm just about to you when I hear you say to the man, 'Well, hmm. I suppose … I suppose to get to the other side?' Just like that. Those exact words."

"Those sound like the exact words."

"That's what you said?" Carl asks. "That's what was so dangerous you couldn't repeat it to me?"

Jerry had lost himself in Jeanine's perspective of his story. The dawn never broke on the danger her repeating the words could mean. And now Carl heard them. And yet, Carl seems more disappointed than overwhelmingly elated to the point of death like the man had been.

"You mean, you don't feel anything weird having heard?" Jerry asks Carl. "No uncontrollable urge to shake and vibrate your body all over the place."

"Not at all. Seems a bunch of nothing."

"And what about you, Jeanine? Does my response to the man have any effect on you?"

"Well, I don't know why you said it," Jeanine says.

"I'll tell you why I said it. I said it because the man asked why the chicken crossed the road. And then something happened. Something odd. My brain thought it quite the entertaining response to say what I said. And it was, I'll admit. I felt … good. Really good. But that's when things went … bad. Really bad."

"I saw. The man started this uncontrolled fit. Is that what you mean? Yes, he was making loud noises. Fell over. Stopped. All those people gathered around, and I couldn't get to you. I hear you tell everyone he's dead. And then I lost you."

All this confuses Jerry. Makes him question what he thinks he knows, what he actually knows, and what he doesn't know. He was confident what he said to the man caused the reaction that led to his death. But here Jeanine and Carl are completely apathetic to it. What was it? The context? The timing? The order in which things happened?

Still, he couldn't deny that the reaction from the man came directly after the words he spoke.

"I killed him," Jerry says. "Dead. Killed him straight dead."

"What?" Jeanine says in disbelief. "You didn't kill him."

"Sure did. Did. My words. I said them. He died. I can't ignore it."

"Jerry," Jeanine reaches out, places her hand on Jerry's that is resting on the table. The warmth of her skin shoots through him with a jolt. "That's ridiculous. Pure coincidence."

"That's what I told him," Carl says. "Words, Jerry, words. That's all they were. They can't move a man to death."

"But you saw him," Jerry says to Jeanine as she pulls her hand away. "His reaction."

"If I had to describe what I saw about his reaction, all I can think is happiness," Jeanine says. "He had the largest smile on his face I'd ever seen. He didn't seem angry. Upset. Livid. Stressed. Paranoid. None of it. Just really, really happy. You can't die from happiness."

"Well, he did. He was so happy he died. Maybe he thought he'd never feel any better than he felt in that moment. Might as well end it all."

"Is that why you ran? You felt responsible. Thought you killed him?"

"Yes."

"But you didn't."

"But I'm pretty sure I did."

"And I'm pretty sure you didn't."

"We'll just have to agree to not agree then. You know, if Carson hadn't fired me, none of this would've happened. That pencil of a man would be alive."

And now Jerry feels it again. A statement. An opinion. An observation. Words that want to protrude from his mouth to bring him joy—possibly the same joy the pencil of the man felt. He wants to hold them back, but he can't. They're begging him. Knocking on the grey matter. Telling him to let it out.

And so he does.

"Carson and that stupid *pen-drawn* mustache."

Jerry smiles some. He feels a little better. An overinflated tire relieved of some pressure. Yes, that is satisfying.

A sound also comes from Jeanine's lips. An odd combination of grunts, similar to the pencil of the man's reaction. To put it in words, it sounds like "Ha-ha".

"Oh, my," Jeanine says. She makes the sound again. Another shake.

No ... No. I've done it again. What was I thinking?

"Jeanine?" Jerry reaches his hand toward her. "Please, not again."

Jeanine looks at him surprised and says, "You're right. That mustache kind of does look like someone took a pen and drew a line above his lip." She blurts another "Ha" and places a hand to her mouth. "What was that?"

"It was the words?" Jerry says.

Carl's eyes dart back and forth. "What did I miss here? Why'd you make that noise?"

"The words, Carl. The words! Are you okay, Jeanine?"

"Yes. I'm fine," Jeanine says. "But that feeling. That understanding that his mustache is a penline but is really just a mustache. The observation. The connection. I've ... I've never felt such a feeling."

This puts Jerry at ease, because despite a reaction similar to the pencil of a man, Jeanine's is more subdued. Controlled.

"It was like being happy," she continues, "but with an increased intensity." Her eyes connect with Jerry's. She squints. Stares. Silent. Awkward. "How did you do that, Jerry? How'd you make me feel that way?"

"I knew it. Words do have an impact!"

"Yes, but I'm not dead. I felt good. Admittedly, the sensation is subsiding. But, still ... how?"

"I simply gave in to what my brain said I should say at the moment. It nudged me. Started earlier today and has gotten increasingly more persistent."

"Well it can't be that powerful," Carl says. "I didn't get that reaction."

"Hmm ... valid point," Jeanine says. "Very valid. But then again, you never met Carson. You've never seen his mustache. You lack the context that makes what Jerry said cause a response." Jeanine's eyebrows lift. Eyes widen. Light bulbs appear to flash inside her head. "Just like when Jerry told the man about the chicken wanting to get to the other side. I didn't respond to it. But that's because I didn't hear what the man asked."

"Like you had to be there?" Jerry says. "For the entire thing." It's suddenly making some sense to him. "You can't react without the full breadth of what is happening."

"Exactly!"

Jerry and Jeanine lean in close to each other, smothered in large smiles at this understanding. As quickly as it happened, the moment causes a spike of discomfort in the familiarity of such closeness, and Jerry snaps his torso to the back of his chair.

"Well, I don't get it," Carl says.

"Of course, you don't," Jeanine says. "And if we tried to explain it to you, it would remove you from the moment further, making the reaction even less likely. You would have to be there, in the moment, to its fullest. Or at the very least, in a retelling of the events, have them told the first time in their exact order and detail. Anything less would be uninteresting. Maybe even boring."

"Ahhh," all three of them say together in unison.

Then there's silence. What do they do now? Nothing they can do. It's all just theory. Speculation. An attempt to make sense of that which doesn't. An attempt to make the illogical, logical. It could all be nonsense.

"You have a gift, Jerry," Jeanine says. "Whatever you stumbled upon is a gift. It should be shared. Others should experience it."

"Are you mad? We don't understand the power of this 'gift'. Not a bit of it. We don't know its power. And quite frankly it killed somebody. We may have just been lucky right now that you're still breathing."

"No. I'm not *mad*." Jeanine takes the statement in stride. She's an understanding and empathetic woman even in the face of a man being disrespectful. Jerry recognizes this immediately, realizes his outburst, his accusation that she may have lost her mind, was his concern that he was losing his.

"I'm sorry. I shouldn't have said that. But you must understand how scary this is. To think that my words have this effect."

"It's a lot to take in. I'm sure." She rises from her seat. "You sleep on it tonight. Think about it. We can talk more tomorrow at work, perhaps during … oh, I'm sorry, Jerry. I completely forgot."

"Well, I didn't," Carl says.

"No problem," Jerry says. "Tomorrow. Tomorrow we talk more while I process this. I'll walk you to the door."

They step right foot, left foot to the front door. Jerry opens the door. Jeanine walks out. Jerry closes the door.

It's 6:00 PM and Jerry's mind is racing a million miles with the things they discussed. Without saying a word, he heads upstairs. Brushes teeth. Removes contacts. Pajamas. Sleeps.

But no, doesn't remove contacts, doesn't sleep, as was mentioned already. He'd not even put on his pajamas. There he laid in bed, staring at the ceiling. Wondered if his words kill. His conscience nagged at him that he was guilty.

"Jerry, someone's knocking," Carl called from another room.

"Well see who it is," Jerry called back.

"Might be that lady from your work again. Not anyone for me."

Jerry had a right mind to set Carl straight. But a left mind to keep it to himself.

"Just answer the door, Carl. It's the least you could do."

"Fine. But I know it's not for me."

A minute passed. Carl's voice again. "Jerry, it's a man and a woman. Detectives."

Detectives?

Detectives could mean one thing. One thing only. Detectives don't show up at people's houses at 8:00 PM or thereabouts to chat and see how things are going. Detectives are looking for

something. Solving something. Searching for a clue.
Like a clue about how a pencil of a man has died.

3

JERRY STOOD AT the evidence desk. He was relieved. Glad to be leaving the station. Especially after he almost killed Adrian. Yes, killed. Splat. Blipped. Cooked, fried, and eaten.

All because of yogurt. Yes, yogurt.

Here's what happened when Jerry learned the detectives arrived at his home.

Jerry places his feet, one-two, on the floor. Sits there. Just sits there.

"Jerry!" Carl yells.

"I'm coming," Jerry calls back.

Down the stairs. To the front door. A front door now closed with two detectives standing inside his home instead of where he wanted them outside, many miles down the street at another location investigating a different situation.

"May I help you?" Jerry says.

There are two of them. A man. A woman. Man seems like he'll tear his clothes if he bends the wrong way. Each contour of his strength lines the button-up shirt with every button buttoned except the unbuttoned top button. He could flex, and an emergency call to a seamstress would have to be made. Woman is his exact opposite in bulk and mass. Matching clothes to the man, including the black slacks. Same unbuttoned button. But deep red wavy hair as opposed to the man's none.

"Yes, you may," the woman says, stepping forward, putting the man behind her. "I'm Detective Adrian, this is Detective Candy.

We'd like to talk to you."

She flashes her badge. Candy does the same. Looks legitimate so far, which Jerry doesn't want.

"Seems odd," Jerry says.

"Odd?" Adrian says.

"Yes. You show up here at 8:00 PM or thereabouts. Detectives. Just want to chat. We've never met."

"I assure you, we're here for more than a chat. You are Jerry Stinson, correct?"

"Am."

"Mr. Stinson, there was an incident today. In town. Not far from where you work. Involved a man named Hom Crayon. You know the man?"

Well, this is a relief. Here Jerry thought they were there about the pencil of the man. To question him for murder. To lock him up for life. Throw the book at him. But they are only there to discuss someone he'd never heard of.

"I'm sorry, never heard of a Hom Crayon. But I will say, it's quite the odd name."

"It's French," Detective Candy says.

"Ahh," Jerry says. "What's it mean?"

"No idea."

"I do," Carl says. "I know French. It means—"

"We believe you do know the man, Mr. Stinson," Adrian says. "Truly do."

"Why's that?" Jerry says.

"Well, for one…" she tilts her head toward Candy, who shrugs. "You didn't bring it?"

"Bring what?" Candy asks.

"The box."

"Why would I bring the box?"

"Because then he'd see our proof. Cooperate more."

"I suppose. Want me to go get the box?"

28

"Don't bother."

"Okay. But if you change your mind…"

Adrian huffs. Brushes a few strays back behind her ear. Straightens her shirt. Smooths her pants. "Anyway, we found a box near Mr. Crayon, Mr. Stinson. Contained three items."

Of course! Jerry smacks himself mentally for forgetting the box of goodies by the dead body of the pencil of the man. He left it right there. On the curb. Waiting to cross the street. A plethora of people witnessing the crime. Witnessing him leaving. Witnesses!

"And you think this box is mine?" Jerry asks. Keeps his composure. Doesn't look surprised. Just stands there, apathetic to it all.

"Yes, we do. Did you lose a box today?"

"What's this all about? You asked me about a Hom Crayon. I said I don't know a man by that name. Now we're talking about a box."

"The box is connected to the man."

"And what is so significant about the man?" Jerry asks this, knowing full well what is so significant about the man. Full well.

"I think I know," Carl says.

"Not now, Carl. Please." He wishes he'd never said a word to Carl. He'll blow the entire thing to bits of dust, scraps of burned paper, demolished buildings.

"The significance of the man," Adrian says, "is that the man is dead. Died right on the street."

Until then, Jerry had hoped beyond hope that his assessment of the man's pulse had been entirely wrong. Dead wrong. But this confirmation was worse to hear than wondering.

"Well, I'm sorry to hear the man is dead. Very sorry."

"The box, Mr. Stinson. Contained three things."

"So?"

"You have any children, Mr. Stinson."

"No."

"Hmm … curious. Maybe we were wrong?" Adrian glances at Candy. Candy shrugs.

Jerry gratefully reflected on the fact that he was single without children. Most times, especially at his age, that would bother him. This time, it could get him off the hook.

"You work at CAF, correct, Mr. Stinson?"

"Actually, no. Just got fired today, in fact."

"We're aware. But you did work there?"

"Yes."

"Because the box was labeled as coming from CAF. When we asked there, a man named Bill Carson recognized the box and the belongings. Told us he fired you. One of the mugs said 'World's Best Dad'. Carson said it was yours."

Of course, Carson would. Of all the people they had to ask, they asked Carson. Was there no end to the turmoil?

"Is the mug yours?" Adrian asks.

Jerry's eyes dart from Adrian to Candy to Carl, who has wisely kept his mouth shut. Maybe he understands the implications. Maybe he realizes he was wrong, and Jerry was right. Turns out words can kill if used correctly.

"Yes," is all Jerry can say. Just "Yes."

"Mr. Stinson, we find it's better in these situations, when we're trying to understand an event, how it played out, how it went down, it's best to ask further details at the station. Not here."

"What? Now? I was just about ready to go to sleep. I was in bed. Staring at the ceiling, so you know."

"Matters like this don't sleep."

"But … I … Please."

"Mr. Stinson, I've also found it's best in these situations to cooperate. I wouldn't normally say this, but a lack of cooperation could be a sign of guilt in some way. A sign of guilt makes detectives question why and look into the matter more. Looking into the matter more might uncover guilt in what we are investigating. Or guilt in another matter. Regardless, you should cooperate."

Jerry sighs, drops his head. Maybe if he had put on his pajamas, they would've been willing to wait until the morning. Perhaps he should've yawned some more. Really played up the act. Maybe he shouldn't have asked Carl to get the door. Ignore it. Let them walk away. Then he could be in his pajamas, staring at the ceiling, worrying if he killed a man with words or not rather than letting detectives come to a conclusion on the question.

"Very well. How does this work? Do I follow you?"

"No. You can ride in the vehicle with us."

"OK. And then you'll return me home when we're done."

"Depending on the outcome, no. You'll need your own ride home."

"I'd rather just drive myself."

"We insist. Cooperation, Mr. Stinson. Cooperation."

"Fine. It'll be fine." Jerry turns toward Carl, calls out, "Carl, you'll be able to pick me up?"

"Depends," Carl says. "When will you be done?"

"When will we be done?" Jerry asks.

"Hard to say," Adrian says.

"Hard to say," Jerry calls.

"Then it's hard for me to say, too. Hey, why not call that lady from your work? She seems nice enough."

Nicer than you for sure, Jerry thinks but keeps to himself.

"Let's go," Jerry says.

"Great."

Hop in the detective car which is surprisingly a lot like a normal car. Turn left. Right. Straight. Red lights. Green lights. Yield here. There. And then he's arrived.

"This way," Adrian says, motioning a hand toward the station's front door. "Now this way." Turn left past the station's desks. Some computers. A few typewriters. Detectives or whoever type

31

away. Looks almost like a bunch of accountants just with lots of papers strewn about instead of neat and even stacks. "And here." She opens a wooden door with a glass panel to a room of cinder blocks painted the color of sky turning to night. "Sit there. We'll be right with you."

Jerry sits at a particleboard table. Chair's padding has flattened to a board. Follows the command. Is cooperative. Best foot forward. Should he ask for a lawyer? That's what they do in all those TV shows. Interrogated with questions when they suddenly realize what they're saying sounds an awful lot like they're guilty. Only then do they say, "I want my lawyer." No one thinks to ask for a lawyer before incriminating themselves. That's what he'll do. He'll ask for his lawyer.

But will that make him sound guilty?

Adrian returns to the room. A room devoid of life. Drab. Dull and other synonyms of such words. Surprisingly, it misses one of those mirrors where Jerry can check his hair, but people on the other side watch him. His every move. Every word.

Candy follows her in. He's eating Greek yogurt. Black cherry. Giant spoon. Scoops a gulp in his mouth. Chews even though yogurt doesn't require chewing. Even the fruity parts that have been mashed into an unrecognizable gelatinous goop.

"Mr. Stinson, thank you for coming here so we can ask you more about this situation," Adrian says. She takes the chair across from Jerry.

"Before we talk," Jerry says, "I would like—

"Yes?"

"To call—

"Yes?" Again.

"My—

Jerry's lips, vocal cords, tongue etc., etc., all refuse to allow the next word to exit. His brain tells him to be smart. Don't ask now. Ask now and you're guilty of something. Ask now, you did

32

something wrong. Ask now, you get the death penalty. An extreme conclusion, but his mind is doing whatever it can to stop the words.

"What I mean is, where's my box of stuff? I didn't see it in the car on the ride here."

"It was in the trunk. Now, with evidence. Not to worry. We'll make sure you get it back as soon as we determine if it is needed evidence or not."

"Evidence of what?"

"Depends on how our conversation here goes."

Candy scoops another batch of yogurt. Swallows it whole this time and sets the container on the table, spoon balanced over the top. The vomit-like odor of the remains wafts to Jerry's nose, which he wiggles to avoid.

"Speaking of the box," Adrian says, "we found it next to Hom Crayon. Who, by all accounts, died right there next to it. Witnesses saw you leave it behind."

"Yes. That is correct," Jerry says. There was no sense in denying the truth.

"But the question remains, 'How did Hom Crayon die?' We found no evidence of a struggle. Entry wounds from a gun or bullet. Nothing."

"Natural causes?" Candy asks.

Adrian turns and stares daggers at Candy. Just stares.

"Sorry," Candy says.

Returning to Jerry, Adrian says, "Any theories, Mr Stinson?"

"This seems an odd question to ask me," Jerry says. "How would I know?"

"Because you were there. Any help would be appreciated. This is an odd case, so it merits some odd questions. Anyway, give me your observations. What happened when you were on the street corner shortly after you were fired? You must've been upset."

The narrative. She was defining the narrative. Angry employee that just lost his job. Looking to take it out on the world. Lashes out at the first person that he interacts with. Things get out of hand. The man dies. The fired employee runs for it.

The problem is Jerry's narrative is no better. Because the words killed. If he recounts the events exactly as they occurred, it could lead to the same result here with Adrian and Candy. That is, if Jeanine's working theory on the words were true.

So, if they were true, Jerry had to do all he could to tell things out of sequence to avoid that result.

"All I know is this," Jerry says. "I answered the man's question. I told him, 'To get to the other side.'"

"The other side of what?"

"The street, naturally."

"Naturally. But what was the question?"

"He asked me why I thought a chicken crossed the road."

"A chicken. Why'd he ask a question like that about a chicken?"

"Because a chicken had just crossed the road."

"It did."

"Did."

"Where'd it come from?"

"A *Chicken House Foods* truck that had pulled over for a minute."

Thankfully, Jerry's plan worked during this volley. The backward nature of the conversation rendered no "Haha" moment. Instead, Adrian's face was twisted in knots. Candy worried more about licking a stray smear of yogurt from his upper lip.

"Is that everything?" Adrian asked.

"Well, he asked me if I had kids on account of the mug. But other than that, yes, that's everything. Our interaction probably topped two minutes."

"And you've never met the man before this encounter?"

"No."

Adrian stands. Paces. Looks at the floor. Mumbles.

Candy stands and says, "I'll be right back. Gotta do something."

Grabs the spoon off the empty Greek yogurt container.

Adrian ignores him. Crosses an arm over and brings the opposite hand up. Strokes her chin. Furrows her brow.

Jerry sits there. Just sits there. Waits for the next question. Wonders if Adrian has to wait for Candy to return before continuing.

"What happened after you answered the man's question?" she asks.

"He lost it. Just went bonkers. Did a haha that went out of control. And then, next thing I know, gone. Lifeless. Dead. He was dead."

"A 'haha'?"

Jerry wants to smack his face. A few times over. The stupidity. The lack of forethought. He never should've mentioned the haha. The haha is the key to understanding it all, and he just handed it over to Adrian.

Ignore the question. Maybe she'll forget.

"What's a haha?"

Maybe not.

"It's just … it's that … it's the noise he made. Sounded like saying 'ha' repeatedly. Admittedly, in different levels of volume and tone, but generally the same type of sound."

"And is this all you can tell me?"

"All I know."

Adrian takes her seat across from Jerry. She blows out a long blast of air like a balloon deflating erratically around the room. The thought gives Jerry a little giddy kick. An increased intensity of happiness. But he swallows it down. He can't allow himself to haha. Especially since it has the potential to kill.

"Well, your help has been appreciated, Mr. Stinson. Maybe Candy was right. Maybe it was just natural causes. We'll see what the medical examiner says. Before you leave, you can pick up your box of three things from the evidence desk."

Jerry feels bad for Adrian. He might hold the answer to why this happened. His brain can't accept the down tone of Adrian's sentences. It wants to do something, say something, that would lift her spirits. Make her forget for a moment the stress of her job. The solving of the case being more important than anything else.

Jerry's eyes dart to the empty container of Greek yogurt. Stare at it. Think about it. And then his brain comes up with the most unique of questions. As before, obvious but not. Expected but not. Ignored. Right in front of everyone's face.

"Weird, you know?" Jerry asks.

"What's that?" Adrian returns.

"Greek yogurt." He nods at the container. She looks toward it. "What do you suppose they call Greek yogurt in Greece? Is it just called yogurt?"

Jerry can't contain himself. His board-straight lips curl. His rate of breath increases, his chest puffs.

But more than him. Because Adrian's demeanor has completely changed. She hahas. A little burst. Eyes wide and elated. She covers her mouth as if the involuntary sounds and movements were unprofessional.

It's not enough. Jerry can't let it go. His brain is telling him to do this. Jeanine is in his head. *It's a gift, Jerry. You need to share this with people.* Jerry is overcome not only with those words but a desire to see the joy. Because their joy becomes his, too.

He continues, "Do you think they call yogurt made here American yogurt in Greece?" He loves it. Absolutely adores it. Why has nobody thought of this type of thing before? He feels so good. So stinking great.

Adrian contorts, snorts, forces her mouth closed which redirects a blast of air through her nostrils. Unable to contain it, her mouth opens, and the hahas begin. Over and over. Grabbing her abdomen. "Haaaa, haaaa! HAAAAA!" So loud. Squeals. Echoes off the walls.

36

She's tipping to her side, grasping the table for control.

Oh, now I've done it! Jerry instantly regrets his pursuit. The good feelings have all gone. He's elicited another death-dealing haha! An anxious knot forms in his stomach.

Adrian tips to the side, soon to collapse to the floor. Jerry jumps from his seat. Glides left. Kneels down. Adrian falls further, the repetitive hahas increase in intensity. Jerry catches her. Prevents a bumped head and bruises.

"Somebody help!" he calls.

This is precisely like the pencil of a man. If Jerry doesn't do something and quick, Adrian will end up exactly like him. A doorstop. Decaying meat. A silent, joyful corpse.

He hates doing it. But it's the only thing he can think of in the moment.

He slaps Adrian in the face. But she continues to haha. Again. Haha. Again. Haha. Candy bursts into the room, another Greek yogurt in hand. Lid torn open. Spoon stuck in like a sword to be removed. Jerry's hand is raised again, ready to unleash another slap. Candy drops the yogurt. It splatters in a fit of creamy white and dark purple magnificence. Three paces to Jerry. Pulls him away from Adrian. She drops a few inches to the floor.

"No, you don't understand!" Jerry yells.

"Oh, I do. I saw you assaulting a detective, buddy. Not good."

Adrian's hahas have settled, signaling the end of her fit. The end of her life. The end.

Her eyes close.

Her breathing slows.

"Adrian?" Candy says. "Adrian?"

Candy releases Jerry. Shuffles over to Adrian. Cradles her head. Taps her some on the cheek. Uses his index and middle fingers. Places them on her neck.

"What is it?" Jerry says. He doesn't want to know but has to know simultaneously. "What is it? Is she, she…"

"She's asleep, I think," Candy says.

As if to confirm his suspicion, Adrian sucks in a long vibrating air, nostrils bassy in their expulsion of a rough sandpapery sound.

"Asleep?"

"Asleep."

"But I thought—

"You need to shut up. Not sure what happened after I left, but I know what happened after I stepped in."

Another hard snore comes from Adrian. Her body jerks and eyes open. Slowly. Then, she forms a smile. A large one.

"Adrian, you okay?" Candy asks.

But her eyes are fixed on Jerry. She smiles. Just smiles. Jerry maintains eye contact for a while but then averts. Shifts around. Smiles nervously.

"What was that?" Adrian finally asks, voice rough. "It felt so ... so good." She lifts herself, wearily sitting back in her chair with Candy at the ready to catch her if she falls at any point. "Oh, I'm exhausted from that. But, wow. Wow! Those words. They did something to me. Made me feel wonderful. Mr. Stinson, what did you do?"

"He slapped you," Candy says. "A few times based on the redness of your cheek. You weren't even fighting back."

"I ... I couldn't." She places a palm on her cheek. "The words. They just made me feel so good. I didn't even feel the slaps."

"Well, he assaulted an officer," Candy says. "We have to—

"No." Adrian puts a hand up. "No. He clearly thought something was wrong. He was trying to stop it."

"Yes," Jerry says. "Yes. That's all. I was trying to stop it. She reacted the same way as that Hom Crayon. I was scared and couldn't think of anything else to do."

"Those words. The yogurt."

"The yogurt?" Candy asks.

"The yogurt. What *do* they call it in Greece?"

"I don't know. I don't speak Greek."

As if their minds are one. Bodies singular in motion. Synchronized swimmers. Clocks adjusted to the exact time, hour, minute, and second. Adrian and Jerry let out a small but brief haha. They look at each other, giant smiles on their faces.

Candy, though, watches them both with a twisted look. This is yet another oddity in what Jerry thinks he understands about the words and reactions. When he's said them and garnered a response, he knew something special was happening with the words. He intended it because it felt right, good. But Candy's expression says the opposite. He made a statement. Simple as that. No intention. No will to cause a haha.

And yet, Candy's words caused the reaction.

For both of them.

But not Candy.

Adrian then glances around the room. Yogurt splattered about like a crime scene waiting to be investigated. She straightens her posture. Smooths out her clothes. Stares straight ahead.

"Mr. Stinson, thank you for your time." She reaches out a hand. "As I said, you can pick up your box at the evidence desk."

"Thank you," Jerry says, shaking her hand.

"Candy, get this mess cleaned up. I can't have all this," she looks at Jerry, raises an eyebrow, "'Greek' yogurt in my interrogation room."

"Yes, of course."

Jerry heads for the door, grateful Adrian is alive, and he's not being put in a cell.

"Oh, Mr. Stinson. One other thing," Adrian says.

"Yes."

"You may be hearing from the CPA. They contacted me, told me to keep them informed about this. It caught their eye, apparently. Not sure what, but you never know with the CPA and of course, we have to cooperate."

"The CPA? Never heard of them."

"Citizen Protection Agency. Global organization. Most people are unaware of them. Law enforcement is though. First time I've ever had to deal with them. Anyway, I'll let them know about our meeting. And, like I said, you might hear from them."

Right when Jerry thinks he's in the clear, he's in the mud. He wishes he understood how to command this thing because it was getting out of control quickly. He had affected three people now. Four if you count Candy using words that caused the haha.

And now Jerry stood at the evidence desk. Relieved. Glad to be leaving the station.

"Name," the clerk at the evidence desk said.

"Stinson. Jerry Stinson."

One minute. The clerk stepped back to a caged room full of goodies. Guns. Rugs. Bicycles. Women's slippers. Men's slippers, too. A stuffed bear. Jerry wasn't sure if they ran a carnival out of the station, and if not, what crime was committed to be holding on to that kind of evidence.

"Here you go," the clerk said. "You know my daughter bought me one of those mugs, too. Kids are great, aren't they?"

"I don't…" Jerry stopped. Thought about it. Got tired of hearing it. What if he allowed the nagging in his brain to commit some words that only he would react to but not someone else? "No. Can't stand them. Can't stand my own kids, in fact."

Jerry smiled.

The clerk frowned.

Interesting.

Now, to get home. Carl was no help. Well, he suggested calling Jeanine. But Jerry doesn't have Jeanine's number. It'll have to be the yellow car with the black checkers.

"Is it possible to get the number for a cab service?" Jerry asked. "And a phone."

Frown still in place, the clerk grunted. Slapped a phone book on the counter, pulled a telephone out from under it, and said, "Have at it."

Flipped through the giant book. Looked under "C" for "Cabs". Couldn't find a thing. Checked "T" for "Taxi". Two services open at 10:00 PM or thereabouts. Picked up the handset. Rotaried the numbers. Someone answered the phone. Ten minutes later, the taxi arrived, which surprisingly looked more like a regular car. Leave. Yield there. Green lights. Red lights. Straight. Left. Turned right. And then he was home.

Jerry paid the driver. Opened the door. And there, standing in front of his home, was Jeanine. Dressed like she's about to go to work at 10:30 PM or thereabouts.

"Jeanine? What are you doing here?" Jerry asked.

"I had to come by," Jeanine said. "Tell you something. A few things, actually."

The unannounced visits weren't Jerry's favorite thing. Didn't even make his top ten favorite. A phone call would've been better. Then again, he wasn't home all evening. So he guessed an unannounced visit made the most sense.

"Well, Carl is probably sleeping. Wouldn't want to wake him."

Jeanine wrapped her arms around in a self-hug. "Well, we can't do it out here. How about we go somewhere? Get coffee. Then I can tell you. Can we do that?"

Jerry wanted to get in his house. Brush teeth. Pajamas. Sleep.

After the evening—the entire day, for that matter—that he'd had, it'd probably be impossible. Might as well indulge whatever it was Jeanine had to say.

"Can."

4

THINGS KEEP COMPOUNDING for Jerry. Another person besides Hom Crayon and Detective Adrian almost died because he couldn't keep his mouth shut. He had to get this entire thing under control. Everything happening to him and others because of him, kept him awake. Past midnight, a new day had started. And he was afraid of what the new day would bring.

Here's what happened after Jerry showed up at his house and agreed to go with Jeanine to get coffee.

Jeanine asks Jerry if he wants to ride with her to the diner. Jerry says no. After all, why would he want to ride all the way to the diner with a beautiful woman, talk and have coffee at the diner, and then drive all the way back from the diner with the same beautiful woman? He was thinking of her. The gas she'd waste. The time she'd also waste.

She knows just the place, so he follows her in his vehicle.

He also realizes how stupid he was not to accept her offer. The chance he wasted to spend extra time with a beautiful woman willing to spend extra time with him.

Straight. Straighter. Turn right. Straight. Left. Merge with traffic. Unmerge. Stop sign. Go. Nearly run a red light to keep up with Jeanine. Two blocks more, and they're at the diner.

The diner is a silver recreational trailer-looking thing. Big red letters above it that say "DIN R" because the lights for the "E" have decided they need a rest. Interior steps back in time. Chrome barstools with plush red padded tops along the bar. Same plushy seats line the entire length of one wall with booths that look out to the street through large windows. About as many customers as you'd expect this time of night, too.

A sign at the entrance says, "Pick Your Seat."

"Have a preference?" Jeanine asks.

"Anywhere will do," Jerry says.

They sit. Server approaches smacking gum on one side of her mouth. Grabs a pen stuck into her beehive hair, notepad from her apron, preps to write. Name tag with embossed letters says "Barb."

"What can I getya?" Barb asks. Mouth opens as far as possible and closes over and over on the gum.

"Cup of decaf," Jeanine says.

"Cup of non-decaf," Jerry says.

"Nothing else?" Barb asks. She's got a fist on a hip.

"Not for me right now," Jeanine says.

"Same," Jerry says.

"I hate the late shift," Barb says.

Barb scoots away, leaving Jeanine and Jerry with a view of a dead town outside. The street corner has a traffic light that changes like it should but without traffic to move.

"So what is it?" Jerry asks. "What did you want to tell me?"

"Right to it then," Jeanine says. "Well, after I left your place, something happened."

"After you left my place, something happened to me, too. Detectives showed up."

"Detectives? It sounds more serious than what I have. Tell me."

"They came asking me about a Hom Crayon."

"Hom Crayon? You know someone by that name."

"I don't. Well, I guess in a way I do. It's the man on the street corner."

"Oh."

"Well, it's confirmed. He's dead. Flatlined. Roadkill. They brought me down to the station. Asked me some questions."

"They think you killed him?"

"Well, I thought they would. But I told them my story. Seems they're just chalking it up to natural causes. At least until the medical examiner report comes in."

Jerry debates telling Jeanine about the yogurt. Figures what can it hurt? Figures he made her haha once already without consequence. Figures she might get a kick out of it.

"Also had an incident."

"What do you mean?"

"Involving yogurt."

"Yogurt?"

"Yeah, Greek yogurt specifically. The detective, Adrian's her name, was done with her questions. Her partner, Candy, loves Greek yogurt. So much that he'll skip out on questioning for a potential murder to get more. He steps out, leaves an empty Greek yogurt container on the table. Black cherry. The grossest one. We're done. I get this question pops into my head. Makes me feel good. And I want to make Adrian feel good. She looked upset due to my answers not solving her problem."

"What was your question?"

"It was—

"One hot decaf, all ready," Barb says. Places the mug in front of Jeanine. Eyes turn to Jerry. "Sorry, hun. Ran out of non-decaf. Will be a few minutes until it's ready."

Jerry has a quarter mind to tell her not to worry about it. He already anticipates trouble sleeping. A mug of non-decaf won't help that situation. He thinks about it too long though, and Barb has gone to another table to take an order.

"The question," Jeanine says.

"Right. So I say, 'What do they call Greek yogurt in Greece? Is it just "yogurt"? What do they call yogurt made here? "American" yogurt.' And she loses it. Hahas like—

"Hahas?"

44

"Yeah. It's the word I came up with to describe the reaction."

"Not bad. Kind of sounds like that."

"Thanks. Anyway, she hahas just like that Hom Crayon. At first, it felt good to have that effect, but then I'm scared. I go over to her, slap her a bunch, hoping it knocks some sense back into her."

"Did it work?"

"Maybe. Don't know. Made her cheek red. But at least she didn't die. And at least she didn't arrest me for assaulting an officer like Candy wanted to do until she stopped him. Hey … you didn't haha when I told you."

They exchange surprised looks.

"Maybe it's the context. The moment. I was too worried about what happened to you to notice the haha. Even thinking of it now, while I can understand why it would cause a haha, I don't feel like I can."

"Interesting."

"Yes, very."

Jerry twists his head around. Looks for Barb. Wonders when the coffee will be ready. No sign of her. No smell of non-decaf reaching his nose either. Only the disguised decaf coming from Jeanine's mug.

Turns back to Jeanine, "What about you? What happened?"

Jeanine takes a sip of her decaf. Steam still rises from it as she slurps. "Well, I went home after visiting you. Didn't do much. Ate dinner. Ironed out my clothes for the next day. Sat on the couch. Read a little bit of DIY magazine. And then it happened?"

"It?"

"Yes. My cat."

"Your cat?"

"My cat. His name is Robert. I have this cat tree I got him two years ago. He loves it. Lays on the top section all the time and sleeps."

"And?"

"He's sleeping up on top. I'm reading my magazine. He's out. Limp. On his stomach. Left paw hanging over the top. His body slides a little toward the edge. Nothing new. I see this all the time. Slides a little more, but he's still hanging on to sleep. Some more, and now there's no stopping it. He falls from the top of the cat tree to the floor. Wakes up mid-drop, gets his feet planted on the carpet. Walks away like nothing happened.

"And despite seeing this ritual many times before I ... hahaed. Just let out a good ten-second one at least. It was the most haha thing I've seen. Especially since it was the only one I've ever seen."

"So something about the moment made you feel it?"

"Yes. That overwhelming joy. So wonderful. But what gets me is that I also felt bad."

"Bad? How so?"

"Well—

"Sorry, hun," Barb juts in on a new stick of gum. "Looks like the coffeemaker's broken. Can't get it going."

"What?" Jerry asks. "Just use the decaf one."

"No way. No mixing decaf with non-decaf. Like I said, 'Sorry, hun.' You want anything else?"

"I guess I'll take a water."

"A water?" Smack, chomp, smack. "Fine. Be back with a water. That won't pay the bills."

"So you felt bad. Go on," Jerry says to Jeanine.

"Well, it's just..." Jeanine sips her decaf. "Normally when that happens, I immediately run to him. Ask him if he's okay."

"And is he ever hurt?"

"Well, no. But that's my first reaction. This time, my first reaction was to feel joy about him falling. It's very confusing. So confusing that once I realized my lack of concern, it caused me to stop my haha. I immediately went over to Robert. Picked him up. Squeezed him. Asked him if everything was okay."

"And was he okay?"

46

"He was fine."

"So where's the harm in that? You hahaed. He's fine. No hurt cat. No hurt feelings. It made you happy. Why worry about it?"

"Maybe. I don't know." Another sip of the decaf. The slurping has turned into gulps. "Hey, I told you the story, and you didn't haha."

"That's probably because I don't like cats. All arrogant. They think they're better than us. You ever notice it looks like they're judging you when they look at you. They get up in high places, like your cat tree, so they can look down on you."

Jeanine hahas. Keeps it under control. "You have a point." The smile stays on her face.

Barb stops by with the water. Ice filled to the brim. Paper-wrapped straw on the table. Smacks her gum. Walks away.

"Odd," Jerry says.

"What?" Jeanine asks.

"You hahaed just now."

"Yes. So."

"Well, the other times this has happened, I had an overwhelming urge to say the thing that would cause the haha. But this time, I only said my actual feelings and thoughts. There was no intention to cause a haha. I've told many people in the past my feelings on cats, and they didn't have that reaction."

"But now I did."

"Yes, you did."

"Hmmm…" they both say in unison.

Jerry rips open the straw. Plunges it into the glass. Sips the water. Cold. Tasteless. Not non-decaf. But he's thirsty, so he sucks it down.

"There was something else you want to tell me?" Jerry asks.

Jeanine comes up for air after finishing her last drop of decaf. "Yes. This entire thing is quite unusual. It's amazing it hasn't been discovered before. I can't help but wonder if you stumbled onto something quite significant."

"Significant?"

"Yes, like maybe something that will change human interaction going forward."

"That would be significant, but let's not get ahead of ourselves. It appears whatever it is kills if wielded without control. So maybe it wipes out the whole of humanity in the wrong hands. Wrong motive."

"That's quite the extreme take."

"But is it? After all, any good discovery by humans usually leads to someone figuring out a way to use it for bad. And unfortunately, I unwittingly used it for bad from the start."

"This is true."

"Yes. It is."

"Hmmm…" they both say in unison.

"Well," Jeanine says, "my point in saying that is also that I think this feeling it gives people is a good thing. Others should know about it."

Jerry sips his water. Pretends it's non-decaf. Pretends it's iced non-decaf. Because regular non-decaf would sear the flesh off the roof of his mouth if he drank it through a straw so quickly.

"Jeanine, I know you're well-meaning. But I've killed one person and almost another."

"Then we'll take it slow." She sits back in the booth, rests her arms along the seat tops. "I have a friend. She works for the paper."

"That's nice."

"I told her about what happened?"

"What?" Jerry nearly spits his imagined iced non-decaf all over the place. "Why would you do that? You told her I killed a man?"

"No, Jerry. Of course not. I still don't think you did."

"But the detectives told me he died."

"Still, I have a hard time believing he died from a haha. Just can't be true. But anyway. I told her about how you told me something that made me haha. I described the feeling to her."

"Did she haha when you told her?"

"No. Not enough context in my description. But she's still curious. Like I said, she works at the paper and wants to ask you some questions about it. Maybe see if you can make her haha. She's been trying for months to move from the editing department to reporting her own stories. Figures this could be the break she needs."

Jerry spins his glass. Looks out to the empty streets. Watches the traffic light go to yellow then red. Watches no traffic reacting to the adjustment.

"I don't know."

"Jerry, this is a chance to make a difference. You want to do this. I know you do."

"Oh yeah. How's that?"

"Because when the urge comes to do it, you're not resisting. You know the response you'll get. It's like you can't help yourself."

"My brain."

"What do you mean?"

"My brain. It tells me to do it. Has this intuition that says it's a good idea. Even with death possibly waiting at the door. It doesn't care. Get the words out. Make someone feel good. Make them feel good even if it kills them."

"Exactly. Well … not the killing part. But that's what I mean."

Barb walks over. Jerry figures she has the world's strongest jaw chomping gum so violently all the time. "Everything good here? You two gonna want anything else?" Smack, smack. Chomp chomp. Chew chew.

And then it hits Jerry again. A simple one. Nothing too complex. His brain knows it. This convinces Jerry it can do no harm. His eyes dart to his glass of imagined iced non-decaf. Which is only water. And he knows it. Jeanine knows it. Barb definitely knows it. But his brain says complain. Complain like you're dissatisfied.

"Well, this non-decaf could be a little stronger. But it'll do."

Jerry smiles at Barb. Feels an urge to squint his eyes playfully. The left corner of his lips lift a little higher than the right. Teeth bared.

"Ha!" Barb says. Just a swift, short burst. Chewed gum flies from her mouth. Rockets in a controlled arc. A basketball flying through the air at the buzzer. Heading for the hoop. Sinking directly into Jerry's glass of imagined iced non-decaf.

It thunks the imagined non-decaf. Splashes like a dropped cannonball. Covers Jerry's face. But Jerry's not upset. Not at all. In fact, this moment is perfect. He couldn't have planned it any better.

Barb and Jeanine both stare at Jerry. Still. Motionless. Mesmerized.

"Well," Jerry says. His brain has more in store for him and Barb and Jeanine. "I'm not sure if that'll make it any better, but I'll give it a shot." He sucks up a gulp of water. Swallows it. "Hmm, not bad."

At this, both Jeanine and Barb burst out with uncontrolled noise. The few customers in the diner turn their attention. Jeanine leans to the side toward the window, the hahas spewing like vomit. Barb loses balance, sits next to Jeanine. Puts her face in her hands.

"Did you see that?" Barb says, but it comes out more like "Di-ha-you-see-ha-ha-ha-that-ha?" Wipes at tears. Pulls them away.

Jeanine has settled, but Barb hasn't. She's still going, nearly falling over in Jeanine's lap. An uncontrolled fit that sobers Jeanine fast. Jerry paralyzes. Why'd he do it again? Why can't he resist?

"Do something," Jerry says. "Do something!"

"Ma'am. Ma'am. I thought … I thought you didn't like working the night shift."

The hahas continue louder with Jeanine's words.

"What's going on out here?" a burly voice asks from behind.

A man steps up. Cook's hat. White shirt. Black and white

checker pants. Full face furrowed with teeth gritted. "Barb, get a hold of yourself."

Barb's eyes land on the man. The hahas vanish as if they never existed. Tears still creep from the eye corners.

"Mel, sorry. Sorry." She exits the booth. Straightens her attire. "I don't know what came over me. He said this … my gum … he drank it. I've … I've never felt so happy in my life."

Mel seems confused by this explanation. Twists his face all up. A pretzel would be jealous of the contortion. "Well, I'm not paying you to socialize. Get back to work."

Barb passes a glance to Jerry. A large smile. That pure joy again. "Maybe the night shift ain't so bad after all." She pulls a stick of gum from her apron. Unwraps it. Sticks it in her mouth for another chomping session. "You folks need anything just let me know."

After she's out of earshot, Jerry says, "That was close. I've seen that now three times in a day." Checks his watch. Not midnight yet. "Yep. A day. Death has been averted twice."

"Oh, stop it," Jeanine says. "She wasn't going to die."

"Was."

"No."

"Yes. I saw the look on your face. You were worried, too."

"Maybe a moment."

"That's all it takes. Even less."

Jeanine bites the corner of her bottom lip. Maybe she's starting to realize how critical all of this is. It's not a game. Cards. Poker. Call a bluff. This is life and death.

"Jerry, at the very least, can you meet with my friend? Indulge her. She asked about meeting tomorrow."

"I don't know. I got things to do. Like looking for a job to support me and Carl."

"Hey, maybe she'll be able to help you with that. Maybe the paper needs a finance guy."

It would be a stroke of exactly what he needs if he could

stumble into a new job the day after being fired. Not to mention, it would show Carl how easy it was if he just put a little effort into things. But then again, does he want word of this thing he can cause to get out? Maybe he stays anonymous.

That's it. Get a new job and stay anonymous. How hard could that be?

"Fine, I'll meet with her. How do I get ahold of her?"

"It's all set up. She said if you were agreeable, to meet her at the restaurant at 5th and Kemper at noon."

With that, Jerry sucks down the last of his imagined non-decaf, forgets that a wad of gum is mixed in with the unmelted ice. That is, until it blocks the path of the fluid. Kind of gross. And he hopes Jeanine forgot it was in there.

Outside in the parking lot, Jeanine says, "You know that gum was still in that water, right?"

She didn't forget.

"Well, have a good night," Jerry says. "Drive safe. Sleep well. I hope Robert does, too, after the fall he took today."

"Thank you."

And that was that. Another life saved. Another death prevented.

Jerry headed home. Two blocks away from the diner. Through the green traffic light. Go. Stop sign. Continued on. Turned around because he missed his turn, forgetting the way he got to the diner following Jeanine. Merged. Unmerged with traffic. Right. Straight. Turned left. Straighter. Straight. And he's home.

Finally brushed his teeth. Finally put on his pajamas. And he laid in bed, contemplating what the new day would bring. How many other people would he make haha? How many other people would find their way to death's door of happiness? Or was it the happiness's door of death?

Jerry didn't know. But he worried that this would-be journalist could be his next victim.

It occurred to Jerry that Jeanine never even told him the would-be journalist's name.

5

IT APPEARED THINGS were getting out of control for Jerry. Yesterday had started so innocently. Now, he found himself in the middle of what he could only surmise was some plot to destroy his life.

Not only did the conversation with the would-be journalist end with questions he had no idea he'd be asking, but now the answers to some of them might be coming to the fore as he returned home.

But wait, that's getting ahead. Here's what happened when Jerry met with the would-be journalist.

Jerry wakes. Sun blares. Blinds him in his own bedroom. It's definitely not close to 6:00 AM. He's not counting the seconds trying to guess the time, either. No, it's much later.

And what's it matter? He's got no job. Nowhere to go. Nothing to do. At least not until close to noon when he's meeting a would-be journalist at a restaurant located at the intersection of two streets. Could it get any vaguer?

Eyes don't want to cooperate. They burn just a little, too. He turns to his clock. The red dot indicates the alarm was set. He must've smacked it off in his half-sleep.

Sits up. Places bare feet on the floor. Sits there. Just sits there. Rubs his eyes slightly. The burning won't go away.

Then he realizes. Ritual: Brush teeth. Remove contacts. Pajamas. Sleep. He missed step two. The contacts still suction to his corneas. For way too long now. Eyes are begging him to take the things out. They need to breathe.

He's done the research before. Sleep with contacts in; don't wear them the next day. Glasses it is. Goes to the bathroom. Priority calls for relieving himself first. Cleans hands. Removes contacts. Grabs his grayish-blue, thick-rimmed glasses off the dresser. Puts them on.

Reminds himself of the time. Looks at the clock. 11:33 AM. Barely enough time to get to 5th and Kemper. Dresses. Out of habit, dons the same clothes he'd wear if he still worked at CAF. Takes the steps downstairs two at a time. TV blares something about naming a price.

"Carl, headed out," Jerry says.

"Looking for a job?" Carl asks back.

"Not yet. How about you?"

"Not."

"Figured as much."

Jerry steps out the door, onto his street. His glasses are a strength too low. Turn a dial, sharpen the image. Nothing like that. But it's good enough to get things done. He's not used to seeing the street at this time of day during the week. A few cars line the curb at intervals. One he doesn't recognize. Black sedan. Four doors. Tinted windows. Super blurry at this distance. Neighbors must have gotten a new vehicle.

Hops in his car. Heads to town. Kind of goes on autopilot. Making turns here and there. Stopping and going. His brain keeps focusing on what he'll say to the would-be journalist. Wonders if it's all a bad idea. Wonders if it's all a good idea. Wonders how he ended up at 5th and Kemper and doesn't remember how.

Parks his car along the curb of the one-way street. Coins in the meter. Quick skip-step forward to the restaurant entrance, which has a large sign on the window that says "HEALTHY RESTAURANT". Steps to the reservation counter.

"May I help you?" a smudge of a man says from behind the counter.

"Yes. I'm here to meet someone."

"You don't know them?"

"Correct. Which is why I'm here to meet them. Not sure if they've arrived."

"Do you have a name, sir?"

"Yes. My name is Jerry. Jerry Stinson."

"No. Do you have a name for the person you are to meet?"

"I don't."

A woman who is Jeanine's friend is all he has. And surely that's not enough information. Unless it is.

"I'm meeting a woman who is a friend of a former coworker named Jeanine."

"Her name is Jeanine?"

"No, the coworker's name is Jeanine."

"Then I still don't have a name."

"Well, maybe see who is here by themselves and find out if they are waiting for me, Jerry Stinson."

The smudgy man gives a judgy look. Huffs. "Fine. I will see. Wait here." He takes off into the restaurant interior.

Jerry uses the moment to glance outside. The blurred traffic moves along at the corner. People going straight. People turning left. Turning right. Honking because someone hasn't moved the second the light turns green. Parked across the street, he spots a vehicle. The smeared view through his glasses could be deceiving him, but the car looks a lot like the one he saw outside his home. Maybe it's a new model getting popular with the masses. Or maybe it's an entirely different car, and his glasses are playing tricks on him.

The smudgy man returns and says, "Sir, I believe we have found the person you are looking for. She says she's waiting for a man who is a coworker of her friend Jeanine. She did not know the man's name, however. But the common name of Jeanine can't be a coincidence. I surmise that this is the woman you are here to

56

meet."

Jerry's brain tickles him. Tells him this man who relayed the information is not only smudgy but has no idea how ridiculous he sounds. So his brain tells him to say something of a remark that insults the man but in a haha manner. So he does it. Does it without regret.

"You, sir, are quite the genius of deductive reasoning coming to that conclusion," Jerry says with a smile.

Rather than stick up his nose. Turn red. Grit teeth. Or consider the situation amusing, curling his mouth, releasing a haha, the man says, "Why, thank you, sir. Please follow me."

This nearly causes Jerry to haha himself since the man's misinterpretation of the statement made him happy and Jerry happy for two completely different reasons. But he stops it and instead follows the smudgy man.

Weave through the tables. Around people stuffing greens and veggies in their mouths. Lots of salads around the place. Colorful-looking dishes. A significant absence of fried foods. Also, the absence of the wonderful odors of fried foods. Odors more like cleaning supplies and sterility.

"Here you go, sir," the smudgy man says, presenting the table and the woman sitting at it. He promptly returns to the place from which he came.

The woman, who was probably in diapers when Jerry graduated high school, sits studious. Clear-rimmed glasses pushed to the top of her nose. Hair pulled back to a ponytail. A smile of hope, positivity, the world is the most wonderful place and I'm gonna make it mine.

"Hello," the woman says, "you're Jeanine's coworker?"

"A day ago, I'd have said yes. Today I say no since I got fired."

"Sorry to hear that."

Jerry sits across from the woman. She holds a yellow notepad. Ballpoint pen. A glass of orange juice sits on the table.

"Thank you."

"My name is Emily, by the way."

"I'm Jerry."

"So, Jerry, Jeanine tells me you have some kind of ability to make people feel super happy." Emily bites the top of her pen.

"It appears so."

"Thank you for coming here today for lunch," the server arrives and interrupts. He's a proper man. Dignified. Black bow tie. Slicked hair. Neatly tied apron around his waist. Not a speck of grease or grime. Not a wrinkle. Without coming up for air, "Our specials today are the kale salad with chicken…"

Jerry kind of trails off his brain, looks at the menu in front of him. He can't keep up with the varied, weird foods named and described. His eyes move about, catching the sandwiches section. Surprisingly, finds a burger in the bunch.

"I'll have the kale salad," Emily says. Looks at Jerry. "Sounds good, doesn't it?"

"And for you, sir?" the server asked.

"Uh, I'll have the burger."

The server clears his throat. "Oh, yes, *the burger*. And the fresh greens with it are satisfactory?"

"Well, in fact, they're not. I'll take the fries."

"The fries?" The server drips the words from his tongue as if he spat dirt from his teeth.

"Yes, the fries."

Without another word, the waiter grabs their menus and turns tail. That's when Jerry realizes he forgot to ask for a coffee. Oh well, he'll catch him the next time around.

"So where were we?" Emily says. "Oh yes, you make great happiness. How do you do it?"

"Well, I … I don't quite know how it works. It just kind of happens."

"OK. So, try me. Make me happy."

58

"Make you happy?"

"Yes."

"It's just ... it doesn't work like that. I can't turn it on or off. My brain decides when to do it."

"So, like, your brain literally tells you?"

"Well, no .. Yeah. I guess. It's very confusing."

Emily makes a face. One of those kinds that says this is a real chore. And all Jerry can think is *Yeah, it's a real chore because you're asking about something not only am I kind of clueless about but that also killed a man.*

"Okay. Give me an example."

"An example?"

"Yes. Tell me a situation where you made someone happy."

"Haha."

"What?"

"I call it a 'haha'."

"Okay. A situation where you made someone 'haha'."

Jerry wishes the server would arrive. Ask a stupid question about overly healthy food. Judge him for getting something unhealthy. Anything to prevent the situation from carrying out. Because if he makes Emily haha, she writes it down, then potentially a lot of people start to learn about this. And that could be a real problem.

Suddenly he realizes he's made a horrible mistake doing this interview.

"I'm sorry. I can't."

"What?"

"I can't tell you. It's too dangerous."

Emily leans in. Focuses on Jerry. "Dangerous?" She writes something on her notepad. "Tell me more."

"It's just that the reaction ... the haha. It's unpredictable. On one occasion..."

"Yes."

"On one occasion—

"One kale salad with chicken special," the server interrupts to Jerry's relief. He places the plate in front of Emily.

"That was fast," Emily says. "Quickest service here, I'll tell you."

He turns to Jerry with a scowl. "And one burger with *fries*." The plate clatters on the table like a coin spinning to a stop. "Can I get you anything else?"

"No, thank you," Emily says.

"This is all I should need," Jerry says.

"Hmph," the server says and leaves.

Emily forks her salad. Brings up a bush of kale, sliver of chicken. Stuffs it in her face. Pulls it in bite by bite like a horse eating hay, slowly drawing in the kale.

Jerry pops two fries in his mouth.

"So what happened on one occasion?" Emily asks.

"Well, it was yesterday. All the occasions are since yesterday. But the first one was a doozy. Which is why I can't tell you. You can't publish this. Word gets out, I could get in trouble."

Jerry picks up the burger, launches his incisors and canines on the bread and meat. Tears it apart. Tongue wraps around it. Tastes the salts and juices. Moves it to the molars. Back and forth, side to side, pulverizing it into a mush that will make it easier for his body to digest.

And prevent choking.

"I can't publish this? But Jeanine said this was something that could change the world."

"True. But she and I don't see eye to eye on the matter. She thinks it's a good thing. I think it's a bad thing. But we both do agree it could change the world."

Emily violently stabs another batch of kale and chicken. Chews it down.

"So, you're really not going to help me?"

"If you had information you thought would be dangerous if shared with people, how willing would you be to reveal it?"

"Very. I want to be a journalist. That's what we do. Right. Wrong. Safe. Dangerous. We are here to reveal the truth."

"Regardless of the consequences."

"Yes. Regardless."

Jerry continues on his lunch. Forgets to ask the server for coffee when he returns to check if he and Emily are enjoying everything. Though, the question seems more directed at Emily. Silence fills the area around them as they finish eating.

"Look," Jerry says. "I'm sorry. I am. I'm torn with which way to go on this."

"It's not like someone died," Emily says. "Jeanine said you make people happy."

Jerry pauses. Thinks. Stutters in his mind. Responds way too slowly to cover over Emily's statement.

"Wait," Emily says. "*Did* someone die?"

Jerry averts his eyes. Looks at the other customers eating carrots and broccoli. Drinking some kind of beverage with little colored balls at the bottom. He doesn't want to lie. But he doesn't want to say the truth either.

"No comment," Jerry says.

"Someone *did* die."

Emily scribbles on her notepad. Makes a hard line under the word she wrote. Bites the end of her pen.

Jerry thinks about standing up and leaving right there. Forget the meal. Make Emily take the check. Thinks about the repercussions of his conclusion. What comes next? Carl knows. Jeanine knows. Now Emily knows. Detective Adrian knows, too, but she thinks it's all just a coincidence. This thing's going to become a fire that he can't control.

"Please," Jerry says without thinking, "don't tell anyone. It was an accident. I didn't mean it."

"An accident. You're saying you said something that made someone so happy that they died?" Her voice raises in volume with each word. At "died," it's a call to attention. A few customers turn their heads. Lowers her voice, "This is … this is exactly what I need. A story so twisted…" She scratches more words onto her notepad. "OK. I get it. Talking about this here probably isn't the best idea. Maybe think about it."

"I don't know."

"Maybe this will help. I've got lunch covered. You can leave now. Tell Jeanine when you're ready, and we can meet at a better spot with more privacy."

Jerry likes the no-pay-for-lunch thing. Helps the halted cash flow that comes with losing a job. Which reminds him…

"Is the finance department hiring at the paper? Jeanine said they might be."

"Not that I'm aware of."

A deal! Strike a deal, and maybe he could get a job. Out of this mess. Move on with his life.

"I'll tell you more. Later. If you can find out. Maybe put in a good word. Jeanine said I was the best they had at CAF. I'm sure I'd do great at the paper. I can—

"Relax." Emily puts a hand up. "I don't even know if there is an opening. And I'm not the one who'd be doing the interview anyway."

"OK. Thank you." Jerry stands. Puts out his hand. "Thank you for lunch also. I hope we can talk again."

Emily takes the offer, shakes his hand. "Me, too."

Jerry weaves back through the tables. Makes his way outside. Stands on the street corner. Remembers the chicken crossing the road. Looks for it. Wonders if it'll return.

Well, of course, not. Not here anyway in an entirely different area. And if it did return? Why?

Walks in the direction of this car. Stops. His blurred vision spots the black sedan across the way again. Doors open. Trunk opens, too. Two men get out. Driver steps to the trunk, closes it without ever looking inside. Both men have suits to match the car. Best posture Jerry's ever seen as they cross the street, ignoring the crosswalk entirely. Headed straight toward the restaurant's entrance.

Emily exits the restaurant. Notepad in hand. She opens her purse. Moves to put it inside.

The men in the suits reach her. She stops. Notepad hovering over the purse. Words are exchanged. They reach into their jackets, pull out what looks like some kind of paper or square something. Jerry doesn't know. At the distance, it's too hard to tell with the stupid glasses he's wearing. They return the item to their jackets. Reach for her notepad. She pulls back. They step forward. Snatch the notepad from her hand. Turn around. Jaywalk to their sedan. Emily yells at them the entire time. The sedan drives off and out of sight.

Emily stands there. Throws her arms up in the air.

Jerry's torn. Does he go and see what that was all about, or does he ignore it? Head home. Waste the day away with Carl. He fumbles the keys in his hands, eyes still on Emily. She twists. Hand to her forehead, nearly facing Jerry.

Eyes spot him. Or he's pretty sure they have anyway. Emily charges forward. A bull. He's a red cape. Right at him. Trying to get the key in the slot. Hop in the driver's seat. Leave trails of black rubber on the road and a hint of smoke.

Doesn't work, though. Emily is on him. "You won't believe what just happened."

Jerry stops the juggling act with the keys. Turns to Emily.
"What?"

"These two guys just came. Took my notepad. Said I can't publish any article about what we discussed. Told me not to talk about it again."

"We didn't discuss much. It's not like you can't recall what I said."

"I'm not upset about that. That notepad was my grocery list. I wrote down what I needed while we talked. There must've been at least twenty things on there! I can't remember them all!"

"So why'd they take the notepad?"

"I guess they thought it had information they didn't want getting out there. Which means whatever is going on is important. Maybe a conspiracy or some kind of cover-up. You ever hear of the CPA?"

"I hadn't. Not until yesterday when Detective Adrian told me about them."

"Detective? You didn't tell me that part."

"That's correct."

"Well, what do you know about the CPA?"

"Only what she told me. They are some kind of global agency. What did she call it? Oh, right," Jerry snaps his fingers, "Citizen Protection Agency. She said most people have never heard of them unless they're in some form of law enforcement."

"Citizen Protection Agency? I really wish I had my notepad."

"What? So you could write it down? It's not that hard to remember. 'C' for Citizen, which we are. 'P' for Protect—"

"No. I just remembered I need to add quinoa to my grocery list. But anyway, the CPA? Kind of a secret organization it sounds like. Emily, what have you stumbled upon here?"

Rather than indulge Emily's use of the third person, Jerry shrugs his shoulders. Puts the key in the lock of his car. Opens the door.

"We need to talk about this more," Emily says. "But I can't now. I have a dentist appointment and a chiropractor appointment to get to. Like I said, me, you, and Jeanine should get together."

There it is again. That bit in his brain. Something was said, and there's a response. Oh, such a great response Jerry's mind says he should vocalize. Put it out for the world to hear, even if Emily is the single audience of the reply.

But he can't. No. He can't. He does, then this would-be journalist is onto it more. And she has the capability of making a lot of others aware of it. Better it stay a rumor. A passing thought. Something a few people know about, but everyone will not understand.

Jerry stares at Emily as all this debate rages in his head. Immovable. Comatose. Paralyzed. In another world.

"Hello?" Emily says. Waves a hand in front of Jerry's face. "Hellloooo?"

Jerry tightens his lips. Nearly bites on them. Clenches his jaws. *No. Don't let the words out.* Tames his tongue. Pushes it down. *Chiropractor. Dentist. Two appointments. If she mixes them up…*

"You okay there?" Emily asks.

Finally, Jerry says, "Yes, fine. But I was just thinking…"

"Yes."

His brain is in control. Wants him to unleash untold elation. Knows it's the right thing to do. The best thing to do.

The curl happens with his mouth. The widening of his eyes. A swelling in his chest.

There's no stopping it.

"Just don't get those appointments mixed up, or you might come out with cracked teeth and a clean back."

Emily stares at him. Just stares. Then her eyes engage. Light up! Her mouth joins Jerry's mouth in a curl. She blurts out a vocal response. Covers her mouth. But can't hold it back. Releases. Lets it all come flying out. There are "Has", "Hes", and "Hos". A bunch of nonsense sounds, but Jerry interprets all of it as happiness.

Jerry's seen this enough to know that if he lets her continue, not only will it draw attention, but it could be detrimental to Emily's well-being. He grabs hold of her in a partial hug. Her body bounces side to side, up and down.

"Hey, let's not forget they took your notepad. You need that grocery list."

Though her haha continues, Jerry feels her body relax. It slows the motion. She exclaims a sigh that starts loud and trails into nothingness. She finally says, "The chiropractor. The dentist. Even if I switch them up, it's not like one would do the other. And, yet, for some reason, the nonsense of the logic made me feel happier than I think I've ever experienced in my life."

Emily steps back from Jerry. Pushes her glasses back up her nose. Stares at him. Again, just stares.

"But if I hadn't calmed you," Jerry says, "that's when things go wrong. Horribly wrong." He steps closer to Emily. Confession time. She has to understand. "I did this yesterday, and the man … it's how the man died."

"Jeanine was right. This … this is amazing. This could change the world.

"Did you hear me? I said a man died."

"How could one die from happiness?"

"Now you sound just like Jeanine and Carl. The words! Whatever they do, they hold the power. They do it!"

"Whatever it is, we need to talk about this. Whatever you discovered has obviously made somebody nervous."

"Yeah, because people die."

"We'll talk. Third time I'm saying it if you're counting. You, me, and Jeanine. See what the three of us can make of this. Decide how to proceed."

Jerry huffs. Why does everyone keep insisting on this being so special that others need to know? Why can't they just leave it alone?

"I'll leave you to your chiropractor dentist," Jerry says. "I have to get home now."

He nods goodbye. Emily does a small wave. Hops in his car and heads home.

Which brings us back to what had made him so nervous. Because when Jerry got home, he spotted the vehicle a block away. Even despite the hazy view through his glasses, he recognized it.

66

Became so familiar with it throughout the day that it was like a close friend.

It was parked just beyond his driveway. Kind of in front of his neighbor's house. Jerry ignored it. Turned into the driveway. Turned off the car. Opened the door. Headed to the house door. Heard two doors open and three doors close. Continued to the door.

"Mr. Stinson," a voice called behind him.

He spun. Faced two men. Black suits. Sunglasses. What did he expect from some kind of secret agency pulling the strings on the world. Very cliche. *Extremely* cliche.

But reality.

"Yes. That's me," Jerry said.

"Ed Aspen. This is Leslie Newman." Ed reached into his suit jacket. Pulled out a wallet. Flipped it open. Flashed what Jerry assumed was an identifier. It said "CPA" in big, orange letters. "CPA. Do you have a moment that we can talk?"

"Actually, I don't. Just lost my job yesterday. Gotta get huntin', you know?"

"Let me rephrase that," Ed said, stepping close to Jerry. "You *will* take a moment to talk."

6

EMILY AND JEANINE entered Jerry's home, bubbling over with excitement. They insisted they had something to tell him that he would love.

But after the past couple of days of one haha thing after another occurring, he would rather have gone up to bed. Brush teeth. Remove contacts, well, not the contacts because he had his glasses on. Pajamas. Stare up at the ceiling. Sleep.

The whole bunch of nothing that occurred when the CPA showed up at his doorstep wasn't helping either. Here's what happened when Jerry had a "talk" with them.

"So let's talk," Jerry says. He steps onto the grass.

Ed steps onto the grass.

Leslie Newman steps onto the grass.

Now they're all standing on the grass. Which Carl never mowed as promised three days ago before any of this nonsense started.

"Out here?" Leslie Newman asks.

"Why not?" Jerry returns.

"Here is as good as any," Ed says.

"Then let's talk," Jerry says.

"We're getting to it," Leslie Newman says.

Ed and Leslie exchange glances through their dark sunglasses. Ed removes his. Reveals sky-colored eyes. Leslie removes his. Reveals mud-colored eyes. Both types of eyes stare back at Jerry. A man walking a dog is a house away, traveling in their direction. Ed's eyes shift to the man. Back to Jerry.

"We could discuss it out here, but these are matters of global security. We'd really hate to alarm anyone unnecessarily. Maybe we can step inside."

Jerry wants the upper hand in this situation. Doesn't want whatever this CPA does to catch him off guard. He'd be perfectly fine sitting at his kitchen table. Prefer it even. But that's too easy. Besides, Carl would probably interject.

"How about my backyard?" Jerry says. "Follow me."

He leads Ed and Leslie to the right side of the house. Red painted fence gate. Lifts the latch. Swings it open. Motions toward the backyard. Ed and Leslie follow the direction. Jerry has the upper hand. He follows behind. Latches the gate.

Backyard has nearly twelve-inch-high grass. They stop in the center, wading in the sea of weeds. Crickets chirp. Snakes most likely slither. Mice skitter about. All bugs and insects short and tall, big and small do their thing.

"I must tell you gentlemen that I've been questioned quite thoroughly recently."

"We're aware," Ed says. "Detective Adrian informed us of your meeting. But we're not satisfied."

"Not satisfied?"

"Yes. Seems to her that it's just a coincidence. You at a street corner. A chicken truck comes out. Chicken crosses the road. You exchange words with Hom Crayon. He collapses."

"Did she tell you the words?"

"She didn't go into detail," Leslie says. "Didn't seem relevant." A pause. "Are they relevant?"

"Of course, they're not relevant," Carl wedges in, standing on the stairs that exit the back of the house.

"Carl, please," Jerry says. "I'm in the middle of something."

"Well, I was getting something to eat from the kitchen. See you three having a conversation. Odd sight. Odd."

"Is. I agree. Is. But still, nobody invited you in on this

conversation."

"No. Wait," Leslie says. "Tell us why the words aren't relevant."

"Don't say anything, Carl," Jerry says.

"Like I told Jerry yesterday," Carl says. "They're not relevant because words can't kill a person."

Jerry grits his teeth. That Carl can sure be a nuisance. Comes right into the conversation like a hot knife through butter, ruining Jerry's chance to shoo these CPA guys away like flies. And now he's said the magic word.

"Kill, you say?" Ed says.

"Kill. That's right."

"What kind of words?"

"All I said," Jerry says, "is that the chicken wanted to get to the other side."

"That's it?"

"That's it."

"I'll admit that sounds harmless."

"See," Carl says. "Words can't do anything."

"We're getting ahead of ourselves," Ed says. "We are the CPA and our duty is to protect all citizens on a global scale. When things like this situation arise, we investigate to ensure their safety is not in peril."

"Sounds like overkill," Carl says. "Plus, never heard of you."

"Most haven't."

"Carl," Jerry says, "they're here for me. Not you."

"They didn't say I couldn't be here. Can I be here while you talk to Jerry?"

"Can," Leslie says.

"Seems like GPA would be better. Global Protection Agency," Jerry says.

"There are two reasons that doesn't work," Ed says. "First, we can't protect the entire globe. That's not our job. Just the citizens. That's it. If a bomb is planned to be detonated in the middle of a forest, we don't care about the squirrels and chipmunks. If a virus is to be unleashed on a snow-covered mountain, we don't care about the bobcats. But if something odd happens to a citizen, like Hom Crayon, or could happen, we're there."

"What's the second reason?"

"The second reason is that GPA was already taken. Now, we have another question about your meeting with Detective Adrian. It appears you told her something about Greek yogurt. And she said she had an odd reaction."

They're getting too close. Jerry wants to divert their focus.

"What about Greek yogurt?" Carl asks.

"Yes, the Greek yogurt," Jerry says. "Just an … ahem … an innocent statement."

"She told us. We didn't understand the point. She seemed to find it quite amusing. Said she felt happier than she ever felt."

"Well, if that's the case, wouldn't your investigation be solved?" Jerry asks.

"What do you mean?"

"If she were happy, it would imply there is no threat to her safety and security."

"Very true." Ed rubs his chin. Thinks.

A rustle in the grass occurs. The stalks sway. Back and forth in one spot that moves along to the left. It catches Leslie's eyes. Then the others. They watch until the seeded tops of the grass stop moving.

"Still, what happened to Hom Crayon," Ed says, "is suspicious. Odd."

"Well, he died," Carl says.

"Yes. 'Died.'"

The stalks of grass shift again. Move directly toward Leslie. Parting left and right, snapping back into place as if a controlled breeze sifted through the unmowed grass. Leslie takes a step sideways to avoid the invisible momentum creator.

"But then we have this other issue." Ed reaches into his suit jacket's inner pocket. "Pulls out a yellow notepad."

"What the dickens!" Leslie calls. He jumps and yells. Skips, hops, leaps around the yard, wiggling his left leg. Slaps at it. "It's in my pants. It's in my pants!"

Leslie bumps into Ed. Ed drops the yellow notepad. It falls into the grass. Leslie's still bouncing around.

Jerry watches all this. Relieved the questioning has stopped. A few hahas well up within his stomach. The scene is nothing like he's seen. Or maybe it is. He recalls a time when he and his elementary school friend, Linus, played in the backyard. A raccoon jumped on Linus. Right on his back. Linus ran all kinds of ways around the yard. The raccoon clawed to his shirt, hung on like a backpack being worn to school.

But when that happened, Jerry worried the raccoon would jump on him. That his friend would be hurt. No part of the situation created a feeling to haha.

But now, watching Leslie bounce around, Jerry was unable to contain himself. Leslie continued uncontrolled, screaming. Shaking his leg until finally, some reptilian creature's shiny, scaly skin poked from the bottom of the left pant leg.

"Get it off! Get it off!"

Ed, seeing the creature, burst a sharp scream also. Like a…

"Like a girl," Jerry said, his brain barely giving a warning. "You screamed like a girl!" Jerry hahaed his heart out.

Finally, Leslie kicks and the creature, a snake if for some reason it has to be said, flies through the air, daring to be a bird and to live amongst the clouds. As quickly as it ascends, it drops into the grass. The stalks sway, move opposite their direction and toward the fence.

Jerry gets himself under control. Hopes the commotion hid his reaction from everyone. Even Carl. Because Carl can't keep his mouth shut. Carl will say something.

"Now, where'd that notepad get to," Ed bends down but stops himself. "Newman, get in that grass and find that notepad since you caused this whole thing."

"No way," Leslie says. "No way. How many more of these things are there?" He catapults to the stairs leading to the house. "I'll stay right here."

"You're useless."

"Carl, this is your mess," Jerry calls. "Get down here and help."

"What do you mean, it's my mess? You live here, too."

"Yeah, well, you've been saying you'd mow the lawn for weeks now. But all you do is watch game shows all day while the rest of us are working."

"Well, you're not working now. You can mow the lawn."

"But I was yesterday. And it's not like I've had time since then."

"Yes, you did. But you chose to sleep until almost noon today."

"You have some nerve."

Jerry spits Carl the evilest look he can conjure, which when observed, would probably just make someone haha. But for Carl, it works.

"Fine," Carl says. "But if I find that snake, I'm throwing it at you."

Leslie jumps at the word snake.

While Ed clears back some of the grass with his foot, Carl gets in the dirt. All fours. Rummages like a starving animal.

"What color was it?" Carl says.

"Yellow," Ed says.

"Oh, then this isn't it." Carl peeks his head out from the grass, lifts an arm. It's balled-up junk mail—grocery ads, unwanted postcards, stuff like that."

"What's all that doing there?" Jerry asks.

"Probably that time I tried to shoot them like a basketball into the cans. I missed."

Carl spelunks back into the grass. The stalks shift and move similar to the snake.

"What's that?!" Carl yells.

Ed jumps back three feet. Single motion. No hesitation. No teeter. Perfectly balanced but now farther from the area where Carl has discovered something.

"Ah, it's just a rock covered in mud. Thought it was a dead mouse."

More shuffling. Some grunts. "Think I found it. Got tucked underneath a bunch of the grass." Carl's arm shoots into the air. Yellow notepad in hand. Ed swipes it without hesitation. Looks it over.

"Yeah, this is it."

"Was there any question?" Jerry says. "Not like we're throwing random notebooks out here all the time." Eyes Carl. "I could be wrong, though."

"You never know," Ed says.

Carl rises from the grass. "You're welcome."

"How about we move over to your patio?" Ed suggests. "That way we avoid another encounter like that."

"If you insist," Jerry says. Jerry would rather be in the grass. Keep Ed and Leslie uncomfortable. Keep him in control. But he also isn't a fan of snakes slithering up his pant leg.

"Now, this notepad. You know where we got it?"

"I assume from Emily. The woman I met today at the restaurant."

"Exactly! She was reluctant to give it up." Ed holds it outward. A prized possession. The answer to all the questions the CPA has. "But this is a matter of global security. We had to know what words you two exchanged."

"Well, that will probably prove difficult, given that nothing she wrote in that notepad related to what we discussed."

"I disagree."

"It's a grocery list."

Ed looks at the notepad. Reads it. "Please. You read this and tell me it's a grocery list. Nobody would make a list like this."

"I assure you someone did."

"Swiss chards. Turnip greens. *Almond milk.*" Ed's eyes twist upward, make contact with Jerry's as if he's reading gibberish and being told it makes sense. "Kale. *Kwinoa.*"

"You mean 'keenwa'," Jerry says.

"What?"

"Q-U-I-N-O-A is pronounced keen-wa. Looks like she got it on the list after all."

"There's no way it's pronounced that way. It's Kwin-o-a." Ed flaps the notepad towards Jerry's face as if he'll slap him with it. "Stop it. It's clear whatever you spoke about, these are code words."

"Code words?"

"Yes. Words used to communicate the information. But we're from the CPA, Stinson. The *C-P-A.* We can't be fooled so easily. Now tell us what these words mean. What you discussed."

"What we discussed is nothing more than what Detective Adrian would've already told you."

"What is kwin-o-a?"

"It's not a code word. And even then I have no idea what keen-wa is. Maybe a rice or vegetable. Something most people don't eat I suppose."

"Stinson," Leslie now interjects. "We know something is going on here. Whatever it is, it affected Detective Adrian. She explained it. Now, we don't understand it completely, but we have reason to believe whatever it was affected her is what got to Hom Crayon. Now that would mean for as harmless as Adrian makes it sound, this thing is actually detrimental to society at large."

"Well put," Ed says.

"Thank you," Leslie says.

"You two need to get to the point," Carl says. "You haven't

asked Jerry any straight questions, and he seems to be under some kind of weird interrogation that is going nowhere."

"Thank you, Carl." Jerry is surprised that Carl came to his defense. Getting him to do anything prompted, let alone unprompted, is usually tricky.

"The point," Ed says, "is keen-wa. Kale. Almond milk. If you don't want to tell us what these really mean, that's your choice. But we will find out."

Jerry thinks of Emily. Her lost grocery list. The disappointment on her face when the CPA took it. He can think of only one thing to do. He'll see her again. She insisted.

"Carl, how's your memory?" Jerry asks.

"As sharp as ever," Carl says. "You know that. Put me on any one of those trivia shows, I'll win every time."

He was correct. Carl's trivial knowledge was so good, Jerry would believe just about anything he said. Except something like human intestines are so long that if you stretched them out they'd circle the earth two times.

"Good. Maybe you can make a career out of it. CPA Aspen."

"Just Aspen," Ed says. "No designation before."

"Really. Not Agent Aspen, Detective Aspen, Special Agent Aspen, Officer Aspen—

"No. None of those."

"OK. Well, maybe I can help you. Can you read off the entire list on the notepad? Carl, can you keep track of the list?"

Carl nods.

Ed nods and says, "Lima beans, Almond Milk, Kale, Legumes, Turnip Greens, *Kwin-o-a*, Avocados, Swiss Chards—

"Chard," Jerry says.

"Huh?"

"Swiss chard. I don't think it's chards. Don't think it has a plural form."

Ed continues, "Swiss *chards*, Chia Seeds, Leeks, Salmon, Ezekiel bread, Lentils—

"Really?"

"Yes, why?"

"Because legumes are already on the list. Lentils are a legume. Actually, odd she'd put the generic term legume instead of something specific."

"You some kind of English professor or botanist or something."

"No. I'm an accountant."

"*Was* an accountant," Carl chimes in.

"Was," Jerry says.

"Anyway, continuing on, Soy Milk, I guess in case the almond milk isn't enough, Trout, Chives, EVOO, and Donuts."

"Doughnuts?"

"Yep. Only normal thing on the list."

"How'd she spell it?"

"D-O-N-U-T-S. Why?"

"Just curious if she used the proper way or trendy way." Some quick math. "Okay. Seventeen items. Not quite the twenty she thought. Got it all, Carl."

"Yep."

"Can you repeat it?"

Carl rattles off all seventeen items like getting it correct will win him a new car or $50,000 cash. He pronounces quinoa wrong, keeps the "s" in "chards" and spells out "donuts". But to his credit, he listed them out precisely as Aspen had.

"That's all of them," Ed says. "What's the point of all of this? You going to tell me something?"

"Nothing to tell," Jerry says. "It's a grocery list. No hidden words. No hidden meanings."

Ed and Leslie eye up Jerry. Look him up and down. Easy enough for Jerry. Silence means he responds accordingly. Doesn't feel pressure to give any other information. Doesn't incriminate himself.

"Very well, Stinson," Ed finally says. "Our investigation will continue. We'll keep an eye on things. As will the CPA's director, Ken James. This has caught his eye. So it's reached the top, and this matter is not closed. Whatever is going on, however people are affected, take it into account. Don't do it anymore. Don't talk about it. Understood?"

"Understood. But honestly, I'm not sure what any of this meeting means. Nothing happened here. We talked in tall grass and discussed another person's grocery list. Hardly seems anything worth worrying about."

"Here's my card." Ed sticks out his hand. Three and a half by two white paper. Printed in yellow ink. Big letters "CPA". Below "Ed Aspen". Below that "OO Investigator".

"What's 'OO' mean?"

"Odd Occurrence."

"Odd Occurrence Investigator. Is that a made-up job position?"

"No."

"Sounds it."

Leslie hands his card to Jerry. Same "CPA". "Leslie Newman" below. And below that "OO Investigator Assistant".

"He's still in training," Ed says. "You have any more to tell us, will you call that number on the card?"

"Will."

"Let's go." Ed walks toward the grass.

"Uh," Leslie says, "mind if we exit through the house."

"Leslie, if you're going to make it in this line of work, you're going to have to deal with a lot worse things than bushes and long snakes. *A lot* worse. Let's go."

Leslie shuffles his feet, steps from the stairs onto the patio. Follows Ed through the grass, feet touching on the tips, knees lifting high until they clear the backyard.

"Thank you, Carl," Jerry says.

"For what?"

"You helped me out there some, surprisingly. Kept them off my case."

"Well, I can't have them arresting you or something. You gotta find a job. You don't, I might be out of a place to live. You know?"

"Know."

They both trudge up the steps and enter the back door into the kitchen. Carl sits at the kitchen table. Grabs an open soda from it, takes down a few gulps, larynx bobbing up and down like a buoy. Jerry makes it to the living room. Goes horizontal on the couch. Stares up at the ceiling. Stares and counts. Counts all the nails he can see covered in paint and spackle that still find a way to show through. Just counts.

It's here we resume, and things take a turn. Time passed. Jerry lost track of how much, but the glow of light from outside and through the windows dimmed. A twinkle.

And someone knocked on the door.

Could have been the detectives. Could have been the CPA. Could have been a pizza delivery guy, though Jerry doubted Carl was motivated enough to place an order for dinner unprompted.

"Jerry, someone's knocking at the door," Carl called. His voice seemed to come from all directions. All directions besides the room with Jerry.

Jerry didn't even respond. Just assumed his role. The door answerer. That's his assignment in his and Carl's roommate relationship.

The knock became rapid. Uncontrolled. As if someone on the other side hammered away, hoping to splinter the wood to gain access.

"I'm coming," Jerry said. Twisted his body. Set his feet on the floor. Stood. Stepped to the door. Turned the knob. Skipped a step. Unlocked the deadbolt. Again, he turned the doorknob. Opened the door.

It was Emily and Jeanine. Big smiles were on their faces. Teeth to bare. Emily's were super white. Not cracked. She stood quite erect.

"You must not have mixed up your appointments," Jerry says.

"Ha!" Emily responds. "Good one. You're right. I didn't. But something happened afterward that you're gonna love."

"Yes, you will," Jeanine said.

"Love?" Jerry asked.

"Absolutely," Jeanine confirmed.

Jerry couldn't help but feel they told him how to feel because they knew the way he would feel after they told him whatever it was they were going to tell him would make him feel anything but love.

7

JERRY GRIPPED THE wheel of his car. White knuckles. Tense. Nervous. He'd never been on television before. Never had a camera staring at his face. Never had to wear makeup to avoid the paleness and splotches on his skin from showing.

But he agreed to this.

Said he would do it.

Here's what happened when Emily and Jeanine showed up, insisting they had news they thought Jerry would love.

"Why do you think I'll love it?" Jerry asks.

"Because," Emily says.

"That's hardly a reason."

Suddenly, Jerry realizes *this* could be something he would love. The paper probably has an opening in finance. Exactly what he wants. Exactly what they want. *Someone to count the beans.* This distracts Jerry more. Why did his brain come up with the phrase counting beans for someone who is an accountant? Seems almost like a haha phrase, but not quite.

"The paper has an opening?" Jerry asks.

"Jerry," Jeanine says, "do we have to stand here right by your door for this conversation, or are you going to let us get comfortable so we can discuss it?"

"Who was it?" Carl enters the room. "Oh, your work friend. Rather, your 'was work' friend. Who are you?"

"I'm Emily."

"Well, nice to meet you, Emily. I'm Carl."

There's this whole awkward stare, a hand extended, a shake that lasts a few seconds past what's acceptable. The two linger in the moment, and Jerry can't stand a moment of it.

"Please, come in. We can sit here." Hand motions to the living room furniture.

Emily sits on the couch. The cushions sink several inches. Carl sits next to her. Same results but his knees lift up higher. Jeanine opts for the reclining chair. A patch of duct tape covers a portion of the left armrest. Jerry doesn't really want to sit next to Carl. He stands.

Just stands there.

"So, is there an opening?"

"Sorry, never had a chance to check," Emily says. "Didn't go back in after my appointments. But I'll look into it."

"Thank you," Jerry says.

"You found a job," Carl says.

"No. Were you listening? She said she hasn't found out if they have the need."

"Still, it'd be nice if you found one that quick. Take the pressure off me, you know."

"I wasn't aware you were feeling any pressure. You two want anything to drink?"

"I'll take some coffee, decaf," Jeanine says.

"Sorry, we don't have decaf," Carl says.

"Well, I suppose non-decaf will do. But just a little."

"Coffeemaker's broke. Dead. Doesn't work."

"Oh, well. I'm fine."

"Me, too," Emily says.

"Your appointments went well, then?" Jerry asks.

"Yeah. Wonderful, actually!"

"No cavities?"

"Nope. X-rays showed nothing."

"I always hate those things," Carl says. "Pictures of the bones.

They won't even stay in the room with you when they take them."

"I know, right?"

"Right."

"Posture better?" Jerry asks.

"All good. Vertebrae are intact."

"Good. Now that that is out of the way, what do you two want to tell me that I'll 'love'?"

Jeanine leans forward, rests her elbows on her hands. "It's for Emily to tell. But I saw it as a good thing when she mentioned it to me."

"Well, it's gotta be better than having the CPA show up at your front door."

"The CPA was here?" Emily asks.

"Yep. Came here asking questions. Questions about your notepad?"

"My notepad! Did they give it to you? I still can't remember everything I put on that shopping list."

"I can," Carl chimes in. Big smile. All glowy and beaming.

"You can? That's wonderful. Can you write it out?"

"Sure. Jerry, you have a notepad?"

Here it is. A remark. Words. He wants to say them. Kind of feels like a haha. Kind of doesn't. Almost feels rude. But satisfying. Jerry's brain pushes him. Nudges him. Straight-up yells in his face.

"Sure, Carl. I carry spare notepads around in my pocket all the time. I'm the Notepad Fairy."

"Really?"

"Yes. I go around spreading notepads to all the people of the land. They bask in the pixie dust of lined yellow sheets and plastic coils."

"Well, I never knew. Do you get paid for that?"

"Of course not, Carl. It's a haha. That's all it was. Completely lost on you, I see."

But not on Emily and Jeanine. They both haha, clearly

understanding that Jerry's nonsensical reply was an exaggeration of statement. A message to communicate the absurdity of the question Carl asked. It's a quick haha from both. No worry of something going out of control.

"So you don't have a notepad?"

"Oh, please. There's probably some paper here somewhere."

Jerry stomps. Through the living room. Forward. In the kitchen. Sink. Left middle drawer. Lots of odd things. Batteries. Rubber bands. Screwdriver. Scraps of paper. Grabs a clean one. Fishes a pen. Closes the drawer. Exits the kitchen. Forward. In the living room.

"Here. Pen, too, in case you forgot you'd need it."

"Thanks!" Carl says. Eyes move to Emily. Toothy smile. "Now for your list."

In silence, they watch Carl write down each word. No hesitation. All covered. Carl hands the sheet to Emily.

"You're a lifesaver. Thank you!" Emily says.

"No problem."

Jerry could insist on relaying his role in Carl even knowing the details of the grocery list. But then he thinks about it. What if Emily takes a liking to Carl? They date. Who knows? Maybe marriage. That could mean Carl moves out. Goes on with his life. Jerry can find a roommate that has a job. Helps pay the bills.

So he says nothing.

"If this is all taken care of now," Jerry says, "can we get to the business of why you're here?"

"Yes, that," Emily says. "So after the CPA took my notepad, I knew we were onto something big. Real big. Change the world big."

"Now you sound like Jeanine."

"Well, I'm right," Jeanine said. "Whatever you have, Jerry, it's done something. Something to both Emily and me. We see things … differently. We're reacting differently."

"Give an example?"

"Well, like the thing with my Robert. And Emily's thing with the dentist."

"The dentist?"

"Like I said, it was wonderful!" Emily says. "Just wonderful!"

"What happened?" Carl asked.

"You'll love this, Jerry," Jeanine says. "Yet another layer to whatever it is you discovered."

"Then tell us," Jerry says.

"OK," Emily says. "After my X-rays, they put me in another waiting room. I waited."

"The room name seems appropriate."

"Yes. Very. Then they called me in for the teeth cleaning. Sat me in the chair. Told me someone would be with me momentarily."

"Nothing out of the ordinary," Carl said.

"Nothing yet. I'm sitting there waiting when—

Jerry's brain does it again. This one isn't so great. But it's still a remark he'd normally not say. Not even think. Not even in the remotest part of all remote parts of his head. But here it is, wanting to come out.

"Seems like they should call that the waiting room instead," Jerry says.

Jeanine bursts a short quip haha. Emily's smile enlarges from what it already was. Carl stares blank-faced, waiting for Emily's next words.

"You're right," Emily says.

"Nothing, Carl?" Jerry asks.

"What do you mean?" Carl says.

"Not even a smile from the … the ha I just said?"

"I didn't recognize the ha."

"Well, I did," Jeanine said.

"Me, too," Emily says.

"Well I don't get it," Carl says. Crosses his arms over his chest.

Resembles a child upset that they have to go to bed without dessert.

"Maybe you're impervious to the ha," Jerry says. "Unable to haha at all. You have no inborn sense of haha."

"Anyway," Emily continues, "I'm sitting there waiting. Bored. I see one of those tanks with the pain relief gas. See the mask."

"You didn't?"

"Did. Put the mask on my face. Turned the valve. Inhaled a deep breath. Not sure why I did it. I'd never considered it before. Maybe I recalled the last time a dentist used it on me. Made me relax. Similar to when you told me that ha."

"You think the gas is related to hahas?"

"I don't know. But I breathe in a good bunch. A big good bunch. Next thing I know, I'm hahaing uncontrollably. Everything in the room is haha. A bird hanging on a branch outside the window, bouncing up and down — haha. The tiles of the floor alternating from beige to white — haha. The assorted tools used to cut and slice inside a patient's mouth — haha."

"The gas made you do this?"

"That's what we think," Jeanine says. "But it never did for her before. Certainly, it never did for me either."

"What did the dentist say when he came in, and you were hahaing like that?"

Jerry's worried. Worried that this haha thing will leave his control. They're happening without him. He can't help but feel he's the cause. Nobody hahaed before that pencil of a man stepped into his life. Nobody talked of such a thing. And now, it's happening at a rapid pace. Affecting, at the very least, those on whom he has unleashed the power.

"The dentist didn't say a word," Emily said. "Took so long for anyone to come into the room, the effect of the gas had worn off. Though, he did say I look unusually happy for someone at the dentist. He probably doesn't get many satisfied smiles, you know?"

"No doubt. So why would I love this?"

"Because it means something, Jerry," Emily wiggles her nose, adjusting her glasses.

"What?"

"Yeah, what?" Carl asks. "I don't get any of this stuff."

"It means you have possibly unlocked something. Jeanine told me about her cat. How she reacted."

"What about her cat?" Carl asks.

Jeanine relays the story. Bit for bit. Straight in order. Exactly what happened. Jerry doesn't haha hearing the account for the second time. He still doesn't like cats. Carl doesn't haha because his brain apparently is incapable of making the connection.

"I don't get it," Carl says.

"It's hard to explain," Jeanine says. "Certainly, we've learned there isn't a rhyme or reason to what makes one haha. Two people can hear the same thing. See the same thing. Have the thing relayed to them. One hahas. One doesn't."

"So we still don't know," Jerry says.

"Know what?"

"Just how dangerous this might be. Everybody is impacted differently. Some are elated, some die, some are clueless like Carl."

They sit there. Silent. No words. Thinking. Trying to uncover the mystery. A mystery Jerry thinks should be locked away, if only his brain would stop making him use the key. A mystery Jeanine is insistent on exposing. A mystery Carl might never experience.

"You know," Jerry says, "this isn't something I love. You haha at the dentist because you inhale some gas. Hardly a loving matter."

"Technically, we're still not to the love part," Jeanine says.

"No, we're not," Emily says.

"So what is it?" Jerry and Carl say in unison.

"The love part is this," Emily says. "When Jeanine told me about this, I thought it would be a story to break. I didn't realize just how important this story would be until I hahaed the first time.

Then I knew."

"I've gathered that," Jerry says.

"But then what happened at the dentist got me thinking more."

"Yes."

"So I have this uncle. The host for the local morning show. Wilbur Munchin. You know, the one that's on during the morning rush?"

"No."

"*Drive at 5*. Really?"

"*Drive at 5*? Why's it called that? This is a TV show?"

"Yes."

"Well, 'Drive at 5' seems like a weird name. People driving into work wouldn't be able to watch it. And if they could, there would probably be accidents left and right during the morning rush. Seems like a disaster waiting to happen."

"It's not for the people driving," Carl says. "It's for the people getting ready to drive."

"How would you know? It's not like you have any reason to be driving anywhere so early in the morning."

"I thought my uncle would find this interesting," Emily says.

Jerry doesn't like where this is going. He's connecting the dots. Thinking of this morning show. How Emily knows the host. Has a special connection. A special connection that would make it very easy for her to convince Uncle Wilbur to do a piece on the haha. *On television.*

"No way. Not doing it."

"I haven't even gotten to the end of the story."

"I know the end of the story. You told Uncle Wilbur about this—

"I just call him Wilbur."

"Fine, you told Wilbur about this. He liked it. Needed something for the show because they probably run out of ideas and news all the time, and he said, 'Sure. Let's do it. Can't hurt anything.' You get the credit for the story. Jumpstart your career. Go straight from paper editor to newsroom video editor. And everyone lives happily ever after."

"Well, that's not the exact way it played out, but yes. Yes. *Drive at 5* would like to interview you about the haha. *Wilbur Munchin* wants to interview you. One of the most popular faces in this town. But the part about using him to help my career is totally off."

"Totally?"

"Totally. I want to make it on my own. Not use my family connections to get there."

"I see." Jerry feels a pit in his stomach. A twist. That uncomfortable moment when words spoken cause pain or anger in another and regret in himself. "I'm sorry. I ... I didn't intend to—

"Don't worry about it. Now, will you do it?"

"I think I already gave you my answer."

"Come on, Jerry. You have something that can change the world. You don't keep something like that to yourself."

"Plenty of people have had something that can change the world. Some guy was smart enough to create a bomb that destroyed thousands of lives. Tens to hundreds of thousands! You think he should've let everyone know about it?"

"Please, Jerry. This isn't that. This is something for good. To help people."

"Of which we don't know the repercussions."

Jerry can see it now. He's interviewed about the haha. Word escapes outside this small circle of those who know. Others learn. Suddenly, people are dropping dead at their bathrooms, sinks, or kitchen tables as they watch *Drive at 5*. Faces splatted in bowls of milk and cereal. Wet hair left undried as a person lays flat on their bathroom tiles.

"Jerry," Jeanine says.

"A man died!" Jerry says. Such a sharp burst. Explosive. He calms. Repeats them with an apologetic tone. "A man died."

"We've been through this before. Yes, a man died. But you're making the assumption the haha is what made him die. How could that even be possible?"

Jerry finally sits. Right on the carpet. The endless movement of feet causing it to feel as if he sits on the wood planks below. He crosses his legs. Puts his hand in his face. There are other consequences to consider.

"The CPA told me not to talk about this. I don't know what authority they have, but I also don't want to find out. I go on television and spew this information, who knows what will happen?"

Everyone sits back. In unison, they release air from their tanks. Stare up at the ceiling. Minds turning gears. Some trying to figure out how to convince Jerry to do the *Drive at 5* interview. Another considering what other defense he has to say why he can't do it. Another not understanding what a haha even is.

Jeanine leans forward. Jaw drops. Closes. Sits back. Forward again. Same routine. Finally, a third time, and this time, words come out.

"Jerry, each time I hahaed, I have felt better than I ever have in my life. I can't imagine not sharing that. Can't imagine denying others the opportunity to feel it. I refuse to think it is a bad thing."

Jeanine exits the chair. Glides toward Jerry. Mimics his seating position on the floor. Right next to him. Jerry's heart booms as her knee brushes against his. She places her hand on his.

"Trust me, Jerry," Jeanine says. "This is something you must do."

He's unsure what it is, but suddenly, Jerry feels safe and warm. Cozy under a blanket. Trusting of all things in the world. He meets Jeanine's eyes. Smile. Warmth.

The tickle in his brain. The nudge. The words. It's doing it again, but not to cause a haha. Not at all. Rather, it's an involuntary response urged by Jeanine. As if her words moved him to act uncontrollably. Granted, more calmly.

"OK," Jerry says. "OK."

"It's settled, then," Emily says. "I'll let Wilbur know."

"What's he going to ask me?"

"Probably similar questions to what I asked you."

"OK."

So it was settled. Emily told Jerry to be at the news station by 4:00 AM. Gave him the address. Jeanine said he should wear semi-casual clothing. Polo shirt. First two of three buttons buttoned from the bottom up. Then, everyone left for the evening. Even Carl. Emily asked him if he'd like to go out to dinner. He said yes. Jerry saw a silver lining in having the place to himself. Carl still hadn't given Jerry the rent, and in a way, Jerry felt his going out for a while was a partial payment.

Brushed teeth. Removed glasses. Went to bed. Set the alarm for 3:00 AM. Hoped to sleep between now and then without fighting covers, nightmares, and lingering thoughts.

And he did.

Did.

Rather than count off the seconds until the alarm sounded, the roaring annoyance blasted from Jerry's right. He twisted out of bed. Showered. Put in his contacts. Walked downstairs to a dark home. Silence. No TV. No Carl in and out of cabinets.

Phone rang. Picked it up. Voice on the other line chirping a tune with more energy than a flock of birds in the morning.

"Jerry Stinson," the voice said.

"Yes."

"Wilbur Munchin. Pleased to meet you. My niece said you agreed to come for the piece this morning."

"Yes. How'd you get my number?"

"We're the news. We have our ways. Great to hear you agreed. Just wanted to confirm. See you shortly." Clickety-click. Line went dead before Jerry could say goodbye.

Showered. Contacts inserted. Brushed teeth. Dressed as Jeanine suggested. Headed out the door. Started the car.

Froze.

Realized he was going on television totally unprepared for this type of event. Uncertain of what to expect.

"What have I agreed to?"

8

CATASTROPHE! DESTRUCTION! ANY other synonyms that comes to mind. That was what Jerry thought of the interview. It was horrible. Just plain despicable. And now he wondered what would come next for him. How far behind was the CPA? Where was Jeanine taking him?

It was all a mess. A horrible, tragic mess. He wished he could change it. Take it all back. Make it so it never happened.

But it did. And here is how it went.

Jerry sits there, frozen, for at least two minutes. Stage fright creeps up on him before he's even seen the stage. An internal boxing match plays out in his mind, and eventually, he gets the TKO, puts the car in drive, and heads toward town.

Though Emily gave him the address, he's seen the station before. Knows the way. Pulls out of the driveway. Heads east. Hits the highway. Soars onto it at top speed. Not a car on the road. Ten miles later, takes the exit ramp. Stops. Turns right. Into the city. Buildings as dark as night with little eyes of light spread across their surfaces.

There's the building. WWLD News. He's not sure what WWLD stands for. "What Would Lilly Do" "Would We Like Donuts" *Yes, yes.* "We Would Like Donuts" It all makes absolutely no sense, so he's guessing his guesses are inaccurate. Though they bring a smile to his face. A self haha, if you will.

Drives just past the building to a parking garage. Grabs the ticket. Circles his way to the top level despite passing plenty of open spots. He knows what he's doing. Delaying the inevitable. Backs into the spot in the open air on top. Mainly does this because when these things get busy, accidents happen. Back out to leave, and *Bam!* Broken taillight. Dented bumper. He's seen it before. Doesn't plan to see it again.

To the garage elevator. Down to the street level. To the front door of WWLD News. But it's not on the first level. There's another elevator. Check in with security. Fill out the visitor's list. Slap on the sticker badge that reads "Hi. My Name is…" with "Jerry Stinson" scratched underneath. Read the menu of offices and suites next to the elevator door. WWLD is floor twelve. Ride the elevator upward.

Doors open to activity. People walking in all directions. Some kind of ticker feed along the far top wall. Spouts out things like, "Nationwide economy growth at 5%." "Stocks expected to rise today." "Job creation at an all-time low." And "Stocks expected to drop today."

Nobody pays Jerry any mind. He stands there.

Just stands there.

He can feel the wind come off those passing him. Blowing papers off desks. There are offices on either side separated by large open windows. The offices have desks. Men in ties. Women in skirts. The men and women also wear other clothes besides those and that complement the other attire. Some look frazzled. Dreary eyes looking for a pillow.

Off to the right, a little meeting area with a refrigerator, table, chairs, and … a coffeemaker. Coffee. Steaming from the pot. Three coffeemakers! All sending evaporating moisture upward. One most likely decaf, but the others precisely what they should be.

Jerry's feet tug and pull, moving him in the direction of the coffee. A man steps in front of him. Blocks his path. A coffee-blocking wall. If Hom Crayon was a pencil of a man, then this guy was the eraser.

"Jerry Stinson?" the man says, staring at Jerry's badge. His beard flows down his neck and never ends as the chest hairs flying from his shirt meet it. He juts a hand out. "Thanks for coming. Wilbur Munchin."

"Hello," Jerry says.

"Follow me," Wilbur says.

He struts forward. Weaves through the people clucking away frantically. Leads Jerry to another elevator. Pushes the up button. Steps in. Jerry follows. Pushes the "13" button. Elevator lifts. Stops. Doors open.

Jerry's not familiar with all the equipment, but it looks like a television studio with several sets. The one directly in front of him says "Drive at 5" on the wall. A couple of chairs rest behind a tall desk. Outside the set are cameras. Some stationed high, some lower, all on mobile contraptions that can be wheeled about the area as needed. The few people in the room wear headsets and stare into monitors that show the focused shots of the cameras on the set.

"And here we are," Wilbur says. "Show starts in about fifteen minutes. Your segment starts about twenty minutes in. Our producer will tell you when to get on stage with me. You ever been on TV before?"

"Haven't."

"Nothing to worry about. Just a few people here. Producer's here. Few crew. Everyone else, including the director, is on the next floor up doing their fancy work. Feels like we're talking to nobody but ourselves once the cameras roll. Just be yourself. Roll with the questions I ask. My niece said this is something special, and I trust her. Smartest person I know. Told me it's about something called a haha."

"Yes, that. Well—"

Wilbur flashes a hand. "Don't tell me. Tell me there." Points to the set. "I like the conversation to flow as smoothly as possible.

The less I know now and the more I learn then, the better the conversation, questions, and reactions. Trust me."

"OK."

"Check in with make-up. By the time they're done, you'll probably be about to go on air. See you soon."

Wilbur takes off to the set. Some people spot-check his hair. He sits at the desk. Starts reviewing some papers. Jerry glances around the room. Looks for the make-up department. Can't find it anywhere. Wanders around the floor. Finds a table with bagels, pastries, and, at long last coffee.

Grabs a cup. Grabs the pot. Pours it into the cup. Takes a sip. Not even hot. Kind of lukewarm. Kind of gross. Not satisfying at all. Sets it down. Picks up a cheese danish. Eats it. Moves it back and forth. Kind of like eating chipped paint.

"You might not want any of those," a woman says from behind. Jerry turns. Her hair is in a bun. Headset on with microphone attached. "They're from yesterday's shows. Caterer hasn't shown up yet today." She puts a hand to her ear. "I'll be right there. Sorry. They need me on set." She rushes away toward Wilbur.

Jerry throws the danish in the trash. Continues aimlessly looking for the make-up department. Finds the restroom. Decides to use it. He'd hate to allow nerves to cause a scene on the air. Finishes up. Washes hands. Heads back out. Another stagehand rushes by.

"Excuse me," Jerry says. "Do you know where…"

They continue past as if he hasn't said a word.

"…the make-up department is?"

"Quiet on the set!" a voice yells out. A few seconds later, "And we're on in 3 … 2 …"

Jerry expects to hear some introductory music play. A fast quip of saxophone, piano. Maybe guitar. But it's silent. Maybe he needs a headset to hear it. The "ON AIR" light illuminates red on the far wall opposite the set.

"Welcome to *Drive at 5*! I'm your host, Wilbur Munchin. We

have a lot going on today in the tri-state area. Here's what we have coming up."

Jerry approaches the set. Not far from some of the monitors the crew watches. On them, a video plays with snippets of the stories to come. One shows a dog walking in a lonely park. Another shows a woman talking and pointing to a manhole on the street. Another is just scenery. That's it. Without the sound, there's no context, which means none of it impacts Jerry.

Kind of like how a ha works.

Jerry stays put for Wilbur's opening monologue. Something about the weather, the mayor, and how he's been in the business for over three decades.

Wilbur says, "Coming up next we have an interview with a local man who can make you haha. What's a haha? Find out when we're back."

"And cut," the director calls.

Everyone kind of sags like wet laundry. Shoulders fall. Smiles drop. Work, work, work!

"Stinson! Where's Stinson!" a woman's voice yells from across the way.

Jerry raises his hand. Turns toward the direction of the woman. She's coming at him. Same woman who told him not to eat the pastries. "I'm right here."

"Great!" she approaches. "Oh. Make-up did a terrible job." Checks her watch. "No time for it. It'll have to do."

"One minute!" another voice calls.

"Right this way, Mr. Stinson." She leads him to the set. Chair opposite Wilbur. "Sit here. Try not to fidget. And, just ... be yourself."

"OK," Jerry says.

Wilbur gives him a nod. Straightens some papers at the table in front of him. Sits back. Squiggly chest hairs push from his shirt like a beast trying to escape.

97

"And we're on in 3 … 2 …"

"We're back. Wilbur Munchin here with Jerry Stinson. Some of you might be wondering, 'Why is he on?' Mr. Stinson here has a unique ability that I've been informed about." Face turns from the camera to Jerry. "Jerry, thanks for being on the show."

"My pleasure," Jerry says. He feels calm, ready to go. He's just a guy in a room with another guy talking to him. A few other people at monitors and cameras. Nobody else in the world can even see him.

"So, Jerry, tell us about this unique ability."

"Well, I suppose it is unique, but it's kind of hard to explain. It's … it's words. Words I find a way to say that make people feel really happy."

"Come on now, Jerry. When my niece mentioned this to me, it's even greater than that. She described it as…" Wilbur shuffles the papers on his desk. Finds one. Looks back to Jerry, "…as a state of euphoria she's never experienced."

"Well, I suppose." A tingle in his stomach tells Jerry to stop relaxing. This interview is putting him on the spot. He's going to be expected to perform. Give a demonstration. The "ON AIR" light blinds his eyes. "But it affects people differently. One might have a state of euphoria, as you said, or they might—

Jerry catches himself. He almost said it. Jerry's an accountant. *Was* an accountant, and the math ends up to: Euphoria + Uncontrolled = Dead.

"Might what?" Wilbur says.

"Nothing … nothing. They might experience nothing."

"I don't understand. How can some enjoy it and others not."

"It's dependent on the individual. Personality. That sort of thing."

"So only people with a certain personality experience it."

"Well, not necessarily in my limited time with this."

Jerry can feel it. Beads of sweat along his brow. One tickles the side of his face. He imagines make-up running down his cheeks in depressing streaks if he had found the make-up department.

"How limited?"

"A few days."

"So if not just personality, what else?"

This is getting way too deep. The CPA said not to talk about this. But here Jerry is talking about it. Spewing the information. Giving it to who knows how many people that watch *Drive at 5*.

"Mr. Stinson, our 250,000 viewers are curious. What besides the personality plays a role?"

250,000? Jerry sees it now. He can't control his brain, which controls his mouth. He says a ha, all across the tri-state area people getting ready for work, eating breakfast, preparing the little ones for school burst out in a series of hahas. All of them drop dead within minutes because nobody is there to stop it. Workers don't show up to work. People don't eat their breakfast. Little ones shout for joy because they don't have to go to school.

"Well, it's also context. If you don't hear or see the context, the words don't have an effect."

"These words, my niece called the reaction from them a 'haha.' Why that name?"

Jerry expects the CPA to barge through the studio door.

"Can you make me haha, Mr. Stinson? Tell me something that makes me euphoric?"

Jerry wipes his brow, wetting his fingertips. Moves to adjust a tie that isn't there. Instead, buttons the top button of his polo shirt.

"It's not that easy."

"Go on. Give it a try. What's the worst that happens?"

The worst that happens is a mass casualty event.

"Sorry. It's just. I don't know. I don't think I can talk about this anymore."

Wilbur has this "ON AIR" face that says "We're on the air, you can't bottle up like this!" His eyes shift to the crew. He gives a nod, as if to say, "I got this under control. Keep rolling."

"I can understand you might be a little nervous. We're on the air. Lots of viewers. Completely understandable."

Jerry's eyes move to the camera. Stare at it. Behind it, a stagehand moves a taller camera system with a set of stairs along the far wall. Parks it in front of the "ON AIR" light, effectively turning off the red glare in Jerry's eyes and stopping more sweat from forming on Jerry's brow.

"Maybe we should take a brief break," Wilbur suggests.

"That would be good."

Wilbur nods to his crew again.

"And we're off," someone says.

Wilbur's shoulders drop. He leans forward. "Not the first time someone was nervous in the studio. Even happens to me. Take a breath. Maybe let's rehearse this. My niece told me something you said about her mixing up her dentist and chiropractor appointments."

Oh no. Jerry's brain wants him to say it again. Those words. The connection. But if he does... He'll simply mix it up. Say it wrong. Fight his brain as best as possible.

"Yeah. Just told her she wouldn't want to mix them up. If she went to the dentist when she meant the chiropractor, then she'd ... she'd..." *Fight it! Fight it!* "...she'd have to hurry to get to the right appointment."

"That's it?"

"That's it."

"You sure?"

"Sure."

"OK." Wilbur sits back in his chair. Shoulders slump. "Well, doesn't seem like I'm in a state of euphoria."

"No. Doesn't."

"No one likes going to the dentist as it is. Not sure what'd there be to be happy about it, anyway."

"I know, right." Jerry feels it. Something new. Recalls what Emily said about the X-ray. What Carl said in conjunction with it. Twists it up. And now it has to come out. "Especially the X-rays."

"What about them?"

"I mean, they sit you down. Put this heavy lead bib over your head. What's all the protection about? Then you have to bite on this weird contraption to position your mouth just right. Most uncomfortable thing."

"Yeah, ha. Yeah, that's true." Wilbur's forming a smile. Leaning forward. Hanging on Jerry's words.

"And then, they're like, 'OK, Mr. Stinson. We're gonna take this picture of your mouth bones now.'"

"Haha," Wilbur slaps the table. "Mouth bones."

"You're like, 'Is this thing safe?' and they say, 'Of course.' And then, they walk out of the room and snap the picture remotely from behind a wall. Like, am I going to die from this picture or something, and they're ducking for cover?" Jerry changes his voice. Makes it a little higher in pitch. "'Oh, don't worry, you'll be just fine, Mr. Stinson. Now I'm going to just run over here and hide behind this wall while this picture beams through your skin to show your mouth bones?'"

That's all that is needed. Jerry's hahaing a little, but Wilbur is howling like a coyote. He bends forward, nearly face down, fist-pounding the top. "It's, haha, so, haha, true. Hahahaha!"

Not just Wilbur. Those of the crew who heard it also have joined in. The studio is pure chaos for thirty seconds. Maybe a minute. And now Jerry's scared out of his wits. He's gotta stop this somehow before he's a mass murderer. But he doesn't know what to do. Maybe a distraction will take them out of it.

Wilbur drops like a rock to the floor. Another crew member sitting in a chair watching the monitor does the same thing.

"Everyone, get a hold of yourselves!" Jerry yells. "Everyone now, or you'll all die!"

But they keep hahaing. It won't stop.

Jerry charges off the set, tips over one of the large studio cameras. It crashes to the floor, scattering a few bits of broken plastic.

"Hey," the woman from earlier says. The smile fades from her face. "What are you doing?"

The others sober up with her outburst. Caught between a haha and concern of something going wrong. Wilbur grabs the table, heaves himself up. Chest pulsating in and out. All his teeth showing. No X-rays required.

"Well, that was something else," Wilbur says. "Now I know why Emily was so excited about it. This is big, Jerry. Big!"

Jerry scans the room. The few people scattered about have come to their senses. Smiling. Content. Happy. To which Jerry is relieved.

The woman from earlier speaks, "You all catch that up there?" She waits.

"Jerry, I gotta hand it to you," Wilbur says. "I honest to goodness thought for a moment the whole thing was a waste of time. But…"

Across the way, one of the crew moves the tall stairway camera thing Jerry saw earlier. Shifts it to the left. Slowly. Parks it. Reveals the "ON AIR" sign. Bright red as it has been. Blasting. Blinding.

"On air?" Jerry says. "On air!" Jerry exclaims. "ON AIR!" Jerry yells. He grabs his head. Looks from the sign to Wilbur. Back to the sign. To Wilbur.

"Hey," the woman crewmember says. "I asked if you guys got all that." She looks to Wilbur. "They're not coming back."

"Do you realize what you've done?" Jerry yells. He's never boiled like this before. He grabs Wilbur by the flaps of his shirt collar. Tugs him close. Anger shoots from his eyes. Burns Wilbur to the crisp. "ON AIR!"

"We, we, we do that sometimes," Wilbur says. Voice shaking.

Jerry hopes he is maybe even wetting his pants. "Guests get nervous. Can't get it out. We make them think we've gone to commercial. Do the interview then."

"How could you?!"

"They usually thank us after."

"Am I thanking you?" Jerry releases Wilbur, gives a slight push.

"Well, no."

"No. I'm not thanking you. Do you know why?" As much as the repercussions of the ha he told have hit him, the scale of the impact hasn't. And then it does. "What about the others?"

"The others?"

"The ones you told me ran the show on the next floor up. Them!"

"The control room? They aren't responding," the woman says. "Control room hasn't confirmed anything."

"How do we get to it?" Jerry asks.

"The elevator," Wilbur says.

Jerry doesn't wait. Doesn't just stand. Doesn't just paralyze himself with fear. People are dying up above, and it's all his fault. He caused this. Wilbur's trick aside, Jerry told the ha. He's responsible.

Words can kill!

At the elevator, Wilbur has caught up. He pushes the button for floor fourteen. Music plays. A happy tune contradicting the scene Jerry expects when the doors open.

"Mr. Stinson, I'm not sure what all this fuss is about," Wilbur says. "It was quite the experience. You—

The doors open to the control room. Monitors show the set on the floor below from different angles. Above them, another "ON AIR" light illuminates the color of death. Panels of controls and chairs surround them.

And the sight Jerry feared. Bodies have fallen to the floor. Still. Quiet. Silent. How many? Jerry can't count. His brain is freezing up. Refusing to acknowledge the sight his eyes feed it.

Thankfully, his eyeballs spot people he can count. Two individuals sit at their consoles of controls. Bent over. One lifts, a big smile on his face. Four others aimlessly appear to be walking around the room. Also showing their teeth. One mumbles what sounds like "mouth bones" another spits out "X-ray" another says "lead vests". The fourth one looks in shock, like he doesn't understand what's going on.

"What happened in here?" Wilbur says.

"Words happened, Wilbur. Words," Jerry says.

"They all just kind of went bonkers," the shocked looking individual says.

"Evan, you okay?" Wilbur asks.

"Yeah. But they all lost it. Mr. Stinson said his piece and the room was mayhem. Yelling. Loud noises. It finally settled down. I don't get it. What happened?"

"Words!" Jerry calls again. "Words! Have you checked their pulses?"

"Their pulses?"

"Yes, the thing that tells you if a person's heart is beating because if it isn't beating it means the life's drained from them completely."

"Well, no, I haven't."

Jerry jumps to action. Glides around the room. A woman is on the floor. Dirty blond hair. Curled in the fetal position. Stricken smile on her face. He places his index and middle fingers on her neck.

"No! No! Check the others. Check for a pulse!"

Wilbur jumps to action. Evan jumps to action.

"Nothing," Wilbur says.

"Nothing here either," Evan says. "Wait … wait … no nothing."

"What's happened?" Wilbur asks.

"What's happened?" Jerry says. "What's happened?" He stomps and clacks over to Wilbur. "I'll tell you what's happened. You tricked me. Tricked me into thinking only you and I were talking. Tricked me into thinking we weren't on the air. And now you've done … made me do it. My brain can't stop it when it thinks it. Makes me vocalize the words. And the words, the words kill."

Wilbur's face flashes white. He looks around the room at the bodies on the floor. Drops to his knees.

"You should've told me," Wilbur says. "You should have said they were dangerous."

"It wasn't dangerous for me," Evan says. "I wasn't even sure what was going on. Felt like they were all in on something they wouldn't tell me about."

"Well we're not going to feel pity for you, Evan," Jerry says. "After all, you're alive. And this thing affects people differently. Like Carl, my roommate. Doesn't phase him whatsoever."

"Do we call the police?" Wilbur asks. "I mean, this is a gruesome scene. They're all dead with these creepy smiles on their faces."

"You think I should switch us to off-air?" Evan asks.

"What?!" Wilbur says. The eraser of a man lunges at an unimaginable speed. Hits a button on the console. "We've been on the air this entire time?"

The "ON AIR" indicator goes black.

"Well, yeah," Jerry says. "Remember how you tricked me? Tricked me into speaking … speaking to your entire audience." The math starts spinning in Jerry's head. "How many crew downstairs and here?"

"With us downstairs, four," Wilbur says, "up here, ten."

"Fourteen total, then. Four dead. Potential for more, but we'll go with that number." Numbers crunch. Spreadsheets of the mind calculate. "That's twenty-eight percent affected with the worst-case scenario." Jerry drops to his knees. Wants to say the grand total but wants to believe it's not true. "Were you exaggerating your audience numbers? 250,000?"

"Well, maybe a little. We're typically just under that. 240. 245 usually. Which—

Wilbur's skin goes another shade lighter. Jerry never imagined there was more than one.

"Twenty-eight percent of 240,000 is…" Jerry thinks, "…67,200 Wilbur. I'm … I'm going to vomit."

Jerry bends forward and lets it fly. Splat. A wave of disgust plasters the control room floor. Droplets bounced upward, spraying the console. Wilbur and Evan join in on the fun. Before long, the control room is a slippery slope of disgusting slop and bile.

"What do I do?" Jerry says. "I … I should've known better. Should've kept my mouth shut. How do I fix this?"

The elevator door dings. Slides open. Men in yellow hazmat suits enter. Big black letters on their fronts say "CPA". Word has already traveled. They know. He spoke when he shouldn't have, and now they're here to get him.

"Everyone evacuate immediately," one of the hazmatted individuals says.

Wilbur, Evan, and Jerry follow the order. As do the other conscious, *living* individuals in the control room. Jerry's thankful. Ed and Leslie didn't show up. He's not being arrested. He's not being questioned. He's being evacuated. If he does this right, he can get out of the building.

And go where?

He's not sure.

But he'll be out of the building. That's progress.

It's a cramped elevator, but fortunately, Jerry makes the first group using it, which includes Wilbur and Evan.

As the elevator descends, Wilbur asks, "You don't really think they're dead, do you? That words can kill like that? I mean, to feel so happy and joyful. It just doesn't seem possible."

Evan says, "What about someone who gets drunk? Or high? They're generally happy and then…" He pulls his index finger against his throat like a knife.

"I hope not," Jerry says. "But the evidence is now overwhelming."

The elevator door opens. The hustle and bustle Jerry stepped into earlier has vanished. Papers are strewn about the floor. Computer monitors flash messages and emails. The offices through the large windows are empty.

And CPA hazmat people have the place covered.

"Right this way," one of them motions toward the other elevator to exit.

They could all be the same person. Same face. Clones just walking around in CPA hazmat suits here to assess the massacre.

Single file. Straight. Past the desks. To the elevator. Enter. Head down. Stand inside the lobby next to the security desk.

"I'm Evan, by the way," Evan says.

"Jerry. Though I think we both know who the other is at this point."

"Well, Mr. Stinson, not sure what'll come of all of this. *Drive at 5* will probably get put on the map, I'd say. Might go national."

"People died, you know."

"Yeah, well, life goes on for those that don't. Can't change what I didn't know would happen."

That's that. Catastrophe! Destruction! And any other synonyms that come to mind.

Jerry didn't even say goodbye. Just exited the WWLD News Building. Went toward the location of yet another elevator at the parking garage. A car pulled up. Screeched to a halt. Stopped right there next to Jerry.

"Jerry!" Jeanine's voice called from the vehicle. "Jerry. Get in."

He looked to Jeanine. Emily was in the front seat.

"Hi Jerry," Carl said, poked his head out from the back passenger side.

Jerry wanted to go to his car. Drive away. Maybe into the sunset. Find another life. Hide from everything here. If he hadn't listened to Jeanine and Emily and to a certain extent, Carl, none of this would've happened.

"I hope you three are happy," Jerry said. "I think I'm about done with all of this." He charged forward. Marched. Stiff, straight back. Eyes with tunnel vision.

"Jerry, please, get in the car," Jeanine said as the car inched along in pace with Jerry. "They're coming."

He stopped. Still looked straight ahead. "Who's coming?"

"The CPA, Jerry. They're after you. You go home, they'll find you."

"She's right, Jerry," Emily said. "Best for you to come with us."

"Jerry," Carl said, "you think this means we can't live in our place anymore."

"Don't know. Don't."

"Yeah, well, if we don't live there anymore, I don't think I'll have to give you rent."

"Come on, Jerry," Jeanine says again.

Perhaps they're right. The CPA was probably waiting to pounce. Those hazmatters were just worker bees there to clean up a mess. The cavalry had yet to arrive. And when they did, they'd want Jerry. If one Hom Crayon can catch their attention, tens of thousands of them definitely will.

He looked behind. The news building was almost a block away. As if to confirm his thoughts, a black sedan pulled up to the front entrance. Two men exited. Even from that distance, it was unmistakable who they were.

"Fine," Jerry said.

Stepped toward the car. Opened the back passenger door. Carl looked at him. Just stared.

"You mind moving over, Carl?"

"I suppose."

Sat in the vehicle. Closed the door. And they sped away, leaving the CPA behind them.

9

IT WAS DARK. Jerry had no idea where he traveled. Who he was with. It all happened so fast. Literally, a blink of an eye. One second, he saw trees and woods around him; the next second, a deathlike void.

But before that happened, Jerry was in the car with Carl, Emily, and Jeanine. Here's what happened.

The city sweeps by in a blur. Like those fake backgrounds that whiz by on TV shows to make it look like a car is moving. Except in this case, the vehicle is moving.

Jeanine's at the wheel. Emily's in the passenger seat. Carl is in the driver's side back seat. That leaves Jerry in the passenger's side back seat.

There. Everyone accounted for. Now Jerry starts wondering. Wondering what happens next. Wondering how Jeanine and Emily ended up at the new building so fast. Wonders how Carl ended up with them.

"Where are we going?" Jerry asks.

"Address that Detective Adrian gave us," Jeanine says.

"Adrian? How'd that happen?"

"We got the time. We can tell you."

The car rumbles ahead and forward. Merges onto the highway going north. This time of morning, all the traffic moves toward the city. They're going away. Cars are spread about like blades of grass in an arid desert.

Jeanine continues, "Carl, you want to start?"

"Carl?" Jerry says.

"I suppose," Carl says. "Happened this morning. Right around five. Phone rings. I'm asleep, naturally."

"Naturally."

"But it won't stop ringing. I yell, 'Jerry, can you get the phone?' Nothing. Yell again. Still nothing. You wouldn't answer."

"Well, because I wasn't home."

"Forgot you had that interview. So the ringing stops. And I dozed off again. But ten seconds later. There it goes. I'm irritated now. Go downstairs. Pick it up. Say, 'This better be good.' And it was."

"Detective Adrian?"

"Detective Adrian."

Jeanine leans over to the left lane, picks up some speed. Passes a little red car. Gray-haired man at the front. Bent forward. Top of his forehead barely clears the top of the steering wheel.

"What'd she want?" Jerry asks.

"She asks for you. So I yell for you. 'Jerry, the phone's for you. Jerry!' Nothing. Absolutely nothing. Silence. Like you weren't there."

"Because I wasn't."

"Well, like I said, I forgot. So I called again, 'Jerry! Jerry!' When you still didn't say anything, I said to Detective Adrian, 'He's not coming. Not sure why.' She says, 'OK. Just tell him to meet me at 7:00 AM.' 'Today?' I ask. 'Today,' she says. She gives me an address. Tells me it's important. Can't talk about it too much on the phone."

"Really?"

"Yes, really. I hung up. Go to your room. You're not there. Then I remember the TV thing you're doing about hahas. Don't know what else to do, so I called Emily."

"Emily?"

"Are you having trouble hearing me? Yes, Emily. She gave me

her number last night after we went out."

It's a sliver of hope in Jerry's dreariness of tragedy. These two are a step closer to Jerry having a new roommate.

If he'll ever be going home again after what happened.

"How'd the interview go?" Emily says.

"You didn't see it?" Jerry asks.

"No," Jeanine says. "Planned to. But once Emily called me, we had to move."

"I told Emily what Detective Adrian said," Carl says.

"Yep, there's a story there," Emily says. "Don't know what yet, but I know for a certainty it's something big. I can feel it. Figured I'd let Jeanine know. We should all go together."

They crest over a hill. Traffic's moving along. Jeanine sticking five over the limit. Right lane. Which Jerry is happy about. No sense drawing attention, getting pulled over, and then the rest is history.

"You all come together," Jerry says. "Even though Adrian only wanted to speak to me."

"Yep," Carl says. "Besides, it's nice to see Emily again."

Emily spins around. Beams a smile. Carl beams. Jerry's kind of sick of the beaming already.

"So how'd you know the CPA was after me?" Jerry asks. "Especially if you didn't see what happened in the interview."

"When we pick up, Carl," Jeanine says, "Emily saw the black sedan."

"Recognized it from when they took my notepad," Emily says.

"It's just sitting there," Jeanine says. "Right there outside your house. Carl comes out. We start moving. That vehicle follows."

"This CPA isn't very subtle," Carl says.

"We made a few crazy turns. Pretty sure we lost them. Then we got to the news building to pick you up."

They've reached a section of the highway. Trees to the right. Conifers. Pine specifically. Both sides. Forest. City is gone behind them. Jeanine takes the next exit. Road bumps along, bumpity bumpity bump.

"So how'd the interview go?"

"Well, it went," Jerry says. "Went about as horrible as you can imagine. Probably all over the place by now. I knew I shouldn't have done it."

"What happened?" Emily asks.

"Well, I told a ha. That's what happened. Couldn't hold it back just like any other time. Not a single statement either. Full blown paragraph."

Red light. Steady halt. Watching the light. Nobody crosses the crosswalk. Jerry wonders if the chicken from what seems like a lifetime ago found its way out here. Maybe it has relatives this way it was going to visit. Pappy Chicken. Sitting on the porch. Chewing on a strand of hay.

"Sounds like Uncle Wilbur will be happy with that," Emily says.

"Well, yeah, he was. But for all the wrong reasons."

"And they are?"

"Well, for one, the crew lost it when I told the ha. And four of them died."

The car momentum adjusts, throws Jerry toward the seat in front of him. He braces for impact. Then he's jolted backward, flat against his seat.

"Died?" Jeanine calls.

"Yes, Jeanine, died. There were fourteen total crew. All of them but one hahaed at what I said. Four of them had no pulse when we checked. The words kill!"

The four of them sit silently. Stare out the windows. Forest surrounds them. A deer grazes along the side of the road. Watches them. Goes back to biting at the weeds and leaves.

"That can't be," Jeanine says. "It can't."

"Can, Jeanine. Can. Saw it with my own eyes. CPA came in nearly immediately. Fortunately, I was able to leave the building before they stopped me. And then you guys pulled up."

Jeanine lets off the brake. Pushes the gas. Car accelerates once again down the paved road. Turns to dirt.

"What about all the people watching?" Carl asks. "You think they were affected, too."

"That's the fear, Carl. That's the fear. *Drive at 5* has about 240,000 viewers. We're talking tens of thousands dead. Not sure how I can live with myself if I find out it's true."

"Well, 240,000 viewers throughout the program," Emily says. "Five to nine it runs. Most between six-thirty and eight. Also depends on the day of the week. Uncle Wilbur told me that before."

"Well, I wish he had told me instead of making me believe I killed all those people. How many between five and six?"

"I don't know. Maybe twenty to forty thousand, if I had to guess."

Quick calculations. Multiply. Carry numbers. Add them up.

"So fifty-five hundred to eleven thousand."

"So not as bad as you thought at first."

"No. But I still don't feel any better."

"Here we are," Jeanine says.

Turn left. Jostle and rock down a narrow dirt road. Reach a house at the end. Maroon vehicle in the driveway with two doors. The front door opens. A woman exits. Detective Adrian, clear as day. Car stops. Jeanine slides the shifter to "P". All exit the vehicle.

"What's all this?" Adrian says. "I was expecting Jerry only."

Jerry feels the need to speak up since the invitation to be here was for him.

"Yes, well. You told Carl. Carl told Emily. Emily told Jeanine. By the way, this is Emily," he points to Emily, "and this is Jeanine."

"Pleased to meet all of you," Adrian says.

"Likewise" and "Same," Jeanine and Emily say, respectively.

"And now we're all here together," Jerry says. "They're aware of the hahas. No secret there."

"Well, I guess it won't hurt," Adrian says. "Come inside. I'll fill you in on why I've asked you to meet me here."

They enter the cabin. Jerry imagines it's a home from a time long past when everybody made their own houses. Cut their own logs. Tarred them. Used an outhouse in the middle of the night. Grew their own food. Died early deaths because the world back then was a wild place. One virus and croak. Gone.

Adrian leads them to the living room. TV is on. A commercial. Something about some medication for some condition that will make things even worse if you experience the shopping list of side effects.

They kind of huddle in a circle. Like Adrian's giving the play. Telling who to go long and whose taking the fake handoff. Except for Carl. Carl's called himself over to the bench.

"So what's this about?" Jerry says.

"Remember the CPA?" Adrian says.

"How could I not? They came and talked to me. They're after me now, I'm pretty sure."

"Well, they talked to me, too. Gave them the info. Decided then to check on what the medical examiner found with the body. Visited the office. And guess what?"

"What?" all three say in unison.

"It was just like that book about that alien who didn't know he was an alien but then realized he was and had to save humanity."

"Never heard of it," Jerry says. "What's the point?"

"The body was gone. Taken. The medical examiner told me the CPA came and confiscated it."

"What?" Jerry says. "Without telling you?"

"Yes. And there's another little tidbit I was able to find out."

"In other news," the TV interjected, "the morning show *Drive at 5* has come under scrutiny after an odd occurrence took place during an interview."

At this point, the words spoken on television grab Jerry's attention. Twist his neck. Shift his eyes. A news anchor sits at a desk. Gray hair and wrinkles display the wear and tear of living life.

"Our own Rory Roebuck is at the scene."

The camera cuts to the outside of the news building. Rory Roebuck gleams his whites. Speaks as if he's been given all authority.

"Thanks, Chuck. I'm outside the WWLD News Building, where a crowd has gathered in response to what aired earlier this morning. During an interview conducted by Wilbur Munchin live on *Drive at 5*, his guest, Jerry Stinson, said something that caused a reaction. Something Wilbur says is called a haha. And these people here," Rory swings around, points to the crowd, "are demanding more. Even though reports are coming through that some have reacted to the words more severely, and they've proven fatal."

The crowd behind Rory bleeds through the microphone. "Make us haha!" "Tell us another one!" and "Give us, Stinson!"

This is worse than Jerry feared. Not only confirmation of more fatalities, but his words are now in demand. In a matter of days, he's gone from an accountant, to not an accountant, to killing someone with words, and now a popular figure in the tri-state area.

"You see, Jerry," Jeanine says, "this is something the world needs. Look at those people."

Is she right? People clamoring for him. Begging for him. Is this what he is supposed to do? It seems impossible. Some get the joy. Some the hahas. Some death. Hardly seems worth the risk.

Rory Roebuck walks toward the crowd. Approaches a man probably Emily's age. Asks into his microphone, "Tell me, sir, why are you here?" Tilts the microphone toward the individual.

"Because, man. Did you see that today? I was getting ready for work this morning. This guy Stinson says something that made so much sense. Crazy true. But he kind of changed it a little. Made me feel really happy about it."

Microphone tilts back to Rory, "And you, ma'am." Shifts the microphone to the woman next to the man. She's got more grays than black in her hair.

"Well, that fine boy. He just made my day. Could barely eat my shredded squares this morning. Been going through such a tough time. Lost my husband recently. Can't tell you what it was, but what that fine boy said about those dentist visits ... made me happy for once in the past month. I don't even think I finished my breakfast!" She hahas a burst. "Oh, there it was again. How fantastic."

Down the line. Rory moves to a child. Boy of maybe ten. Jerry assumes the woman next to him is his mother. "And how about you, son?" Rory asks. "What brings you here?"

The little boy talks in a sheepish voice. "My mom told me to get dressed for school because I woke up so early. Then she said I couldn't play video games. Then she made weird noises. And now I'm here. I don't have to go to school today!"

Rory steps away from the crowd. Back to the camera. "And there you have it. People of all ages and genders, here this morning at the WWLD News Building. All looking for another haha. But the CPA, which I'm told is an organization called the Citizen Protection Agency, has sealed off access to the building. Rumor is that some in the studio may have had a fatal reaction to the haha. We're waiting to—"

"Turn it off," Jerry says. "I don't want to hear it."

Adrian turns the channel instead of shutting it off. It's another news report. "BREAKING" scrolls along the bottom of the screen. She says, "But that's the thing I wanted to tell you that the medical examiner discovered."

"We're on with Dr. Bergen Beckenbauer," the news anchor says on the left side of the screen. Perfectly parted dark hair, winning smile, winning dimples. "Dr. Beckenbauer, thank you for being with us on such short notice."

"My pleasure," Dr. Beckenbaeur says on the ride side of the screen. Disheveled gray hair, losing grimace, absolutely no dimples.

"What do you make of this reaction people have to the interview with Jerry Stinson this morning?"

"Well, in my assessment, having learned of this within the past hour, I can't help but wonder if this is some form of attack. A verbal virus, if you will. The accounts I'm hearing are some people feel joy. Others, though, have died. Still others are asymptomatic. It has all the likings of some sort of disease. Albeit one spread through the use of these words."

"Do you think we're in danger?"

"In my humble opinion, it's too early to tell. But it's good to err on the side of caution."

"A virus?" Carl says. "That's a new one. Maybe there's something to this."

"Can we turn this off?" Jerry asks yet again. "I can't keep hearing this nonsense."

Adrian pushes a button on the TV. Switches to yet another channel to Jerry's irritation. Immediately, a voice booms, "And this is getting out of control! Whatever this Stinson character did, it's already changing people." This man is nearly yelling. Boisterous. Over-the-top. "We have a caller on the phone. Sherry, you're on the air. Tell us what you saw."

"Hey, Phil," Sherry says. Sounds like someone who quit smoking a little too late. "I'm drove into work this morning. Not far from the WWLD News Building. There's this person walking down the street. Maybe half a block from the crowd. Tripped on the leg of a bench because they weren't paying attention. Tumbled forward. Fell flat on their back. I stopped immediately to see if they were okay."

"Like any good citizen would do," Phil says. "But what'd you see after that?"

"Well, some of the crowd, they saw it, too. But they didn't help.

Instead, they all just did this haha thing. Just hahaed so much. The guy stood up. I went to check on him."

"Was he okay?"

"Yeah, he was fine. But he could've been badly hurt, and they were all hahaing. They were so happy about it. It was sick, really."

"Thank you, caller, for that eyewitness account. Those watching might think all this is ridiculous. And it may be. But according to my sources, the CPA, some global protection organization, has confiscated all video documentation of the interview on *Drive at 5*, preventing anyone from seeing it again."

Jerry had, to that point, kept his cool. But Adrian's refusal to power off the television hits him. He'd usually hold back. Stuff it down. Keep it to himself. But his brain. Oh wow! His brain. It allows the angry bits to ooze through.

"WOULD YOU JUST SHUT IT OFF! I'm tired of hearing this. I can't."

That stuns them to paralysis. Dropped jaws. Silent gapes. After a moment without response, television still roaring on about the hahas, Adrian moves forward.

"Mr. Stinson, I would turn it off, but the TV's power button doesn't work. It's dead."

"Dead?" Jerry says. How could he allow the outburst? The foolishness? "Sorry, I didn't know. Well, what about lowering the volume?"

"Also broken."

"Could you … you know … unplug it?"

"I could, but then I won't be able to turn it on to watch it."

"So you just leave it on all the time," Carl chimes in. "Makes sense if you want to make sure to watch TV. Hey, maybe put it on channel twelve. They should be showing a game show now instead of news."

Adrian changes the channel. Lands it on twelve. Sure enough, a host is on the screen, holding a microphone. A contestant stands

119

next to him. A large dial device there. Spin it. Win the car. Win the $25,000. Or lose, of course. Most likely scenario.

Carl's eyes rove to Jerry. "Does that work for you, Jerry?"

"I … Works. Works. Thank you, Carl."

"OK," Adrian says. "Where were we?"

"You were saying," Emily says. Wiggles the glasses on her nose. "About the medical examiner?"

"Right," Adrian says. "So she tells me she only had a few moments with the body before the CPA took it. But Hom Crayon, he looked so peaceful to her. And then, and she swears, his lower jaw moved. Closed ever so slightly from that gaping smile he had when he died. She bends down. Gets close. Feels a little wind against her face. Just the slightest amount."

"Wind?" Jerry says. "What do you mean?"

"From his mouth, Jerry!" Jeanine says. "Go on, Detective."

"Sure," Adrian says. "Then she places the index and middle fingers on his neck. Nothing for a good ten or fifteen seconds. Then, she said anyway, a bump."

"A bump?" Jerry questions. "What's that mean? Like, a heartbeat?"

"That's what she said."

"Impossible. That man was dead."

"Maybe he wasn't," Jeanine says. "The words can't kill, Jerry. I'm sure of it."

"As am I," Carl says. "Words, Jerry, words. A tree falling on a man, that kills. Not words."

"This is the story of the century! The millennium maybe," Emily says. "Stumbled right onto a world-changing event and some kind of government cover-up."

"I'm glad you find this so entertaining," Jerry says. "Because I don't. I'm not sure what to think."

This is how Jerry ended up where he was. He stormed from the room. A dark gray cloud. A few lightning bolts. A rumble of thunder. Toward the back door that came off the kitchen. Squeaked open like a squealing mouse. Slammed shut on its own.

Outside. The smell of pine. A forest of forever in front of him. No worries. No concerns. Just run right out in those trees. Never look back. Never talk to anyone again. Never tell another ha. That would solve this quickly.

He steps forward. Another step.

There could be bears. A bear might eat him. Maybe mountain lions, too. They'd claw him. Bears would claw him, too. Then they'd both eat him. Maybe fight over who gets what part.

Maybe running away wasn't the best idea.

Now calmed, Jerry turned back toward the house. Stared at it. Wondered if he was doomed to hide like a fugitive here so that neither the police, the CPA, or his newfound fandom could find him.

It was then that the sun was stolen from Jerry. A dark cloth impenetrable by the eyes covered his face. He was grabbed under each armpit. Dragged along the dirt and leaves. He kicked his feet, pushed, dug them into the ground. Whoever had him had him good. Real good.

He yelled out, "Help! Help!"

The only return he received was the blaring television in Detective Adrian's place. Something about the hahas. Nothing from Adrian, Carl, Emily, or even Jeanine.

Thrown forward. Landed on a cushy seat. Clink and clank of a door closing. Another behind him opened. Someone sighed. Driver door opened. Door behind him, the trunk Jerry deduced, closed. Driver door closed. Vibration and rumble, odor of exhaust. Bumped down the driveway to where his captors had decided to take him.

10

JERRY'S EARS HAD had enough. One could put up with all kinds of annoying sounds. But as he sat waiting in the Director's office, listening to the blaring noise, he was on the verge of insanity. Locked in the rubber room with rats.

But before he reached that point, he had endured a boring excursion to "who knows where". One of those places you can never reach again and worry how you'll get back.

Here's what happened to Jerry after a bag was placed on his head, and he was put into a vehicle that sped away.

Jerry's never been kidnapped before. Never had a sack put over his head. Never rode anywhere in darkness. He wasn't sure how a kidnap victim should act, but he knows this:

He doesn't like it.

"Who are you? Where are you taking me?"

Unless the vehicle drives itself, his captors refuse to answer.

He wishes he had spy training. Study the turns even in the dark. Going straight for a long time. A long time. Maybe an hour. He dozes. Wakes. Isn't sure if they've been going straight the entire time or not. Vehicle slows. Shifts rightways. Stops. Goes Left. Continues. Soon, Jerry's forgotten the turns as he tries to remember the next ones that come.

Oh, forget it. He realizes he'll never figure out where he is.

"Where are you taking me?" Jerry asks again.

"We're almost there," a man's voice returns. Either he remembers, or his mind convinces him, but he's fairly certain it is

Ed.

"Ed? Leslie?"

"Yeah," Leslie responds.

"Quiet," Ed says. "Told you not to confirm it's us."

"Well, now you've both confirmed it," Jerry says. "I'll ask again. Where are you taking me?"

"Won't be much longer," Ed says.

Jerry's brain gives him a bright idea. A great idea, in fact. And really, it's not even his brain. It's his body. Just needs to do its daily-multiple times daily routine.

"Well, I have to pee. Unless it's five minutes, can we make a stop?"

"Try to hold it."

"I really can't."

"Well, try."

"Can't. Bound to let it go all over your back seat here. This government issue?"

"In a manner of speaking."

"Does the in-a-manner-of-speaking-government like people urinating on their property?"

"They're not too fond of it. Fine. You have two minutes."

Car slows. Eases right, by Jerry's motion detection. Stops. Trunk pops open like before, to which Ed blurts a frustrated tone. Back passenger side door opens. Leslie says, "Come on."

Jerry scoots toward the door. Day still dark as night. A hand grabs his elbow. Helps him out.

"I can do this myself, you know," Jerry says.

The hand let's go.

"But I do need to see what I'm doing."

A few seconds of silence. Ed says, "Go ahead. We'll put it back on when he's done."

Bag removed. Daylight pours into Jerry's eyes. Squints. Grass as tall as that in his backyard spreads out on a field that reaches in each direction. No mountains. No houses. Absolutely bonkers isolation.

"There's not even a tree here," Jerry says. "Nowhere to go."

"Just head out into the grass a ways," Leslie says. "We won't see you. Watch out for any snakes."

Jerry sighs. Trudges forward. He'd hoped he'd have an idea of his location. But this gives him nothing. He also had planned to relieve himself and run in a direction to hide afterward. The plan could still happen. But he had nowhere but tall grass to go to. Leslie would probably stay back instead of chase. Even then, Ed would follow the path of trampled grass blades.

So, no escape. That much he knows. Walks out ten yards or so. Relieves himself—carefully—to avoid the need to wash his hands. Walks back. Leslie places the bag back on his head.

"Is that still necessary?" Jerry asks.

"Yes," Ed says. "Can't have you knowing where this place is located. Top secret stuff, which you've kind of shined a light on."

"I think it's shone."

"Pretty sure it's shined."

Back in the car. Sit and wait and wait. Finally pulls to a stop. Doors open. Exit car. Walked from outdoors to indoors. Right. Straight. Stop. Some beeping sounds. Left. Left. Door creaks open.

"Sit here," Ed says. Pulls the bag off Jerry's head.

It's a room. Not one he expected, though. Plush carpeting. A leather sofa to the right. The desk opposite the sofa is some fancy wood and a fancy size. The desk of someone important. Pale green rotary phone. Various plaques and awards on the wall.

It hits Jerry, as he examines the room. Makes the wheels in his brain spin. The situation is clearly serious. Something to do with what happened on *Drive at 5*. But he wants to make it about something else. Say it's something unrelated. Unexpected.

"I don't need to see a therapist," Jerry says before he has a chance to think about the words. Smiles to himself.

"That one of your hahas?" Ed asks.

"Kind of."

"Well, it didn't work on me."

"I can tell. This your office?"

"I'll ask the questions, Jerry." He nods to Leslie. "You can go. Get the Director. Let him know we're here."

Leslie exits. As requested, Jerry sits on the leather sofa. Direct middle. Position keeps his knees high, like an adult sitting at a children's desk at school.

Ed shifts over to the important person's desk. Leans against it. Uses it like a chair. Folds his arms on his chest.

"We told you not to talk about this, Jerry. It wasn't an idle threat."

"I didn't plan to."

"But you did."

"Did.

"And now look what you've done. Have you seen the news?"

"Have."

Ed steps away from the desk. Goes to the window. Rays of light shine through like prison bars. "We let you off way too easy. I should've known better. So why'd you talk?"

Lots of reasons there. He could easily blame Emily or Carl or Jeanine. Tell Ed they convinced him it was the right thing to do. He could say that Jeanine seems to have this way of making him feel all warm and fuzzy, and he'd jump off a bridge if she asked him to. He could also say it's beyond his control.

But is it?

Yes, his brain nudges him. Pushes him. Gets him to the precipice of that bridge. But also, he wants it. He has to say it. This all started because of him.

"It kind of happens. The interview was set up. I had every intention of not telling a ha."

"A ha?"

125

"It's what I call it when I know I'm saying something that will make someone haha. Anyway, something happens. The individual says something, and my brain … it makes this connection—

"Aspen, I'll take it from here."

Both Jerry's and Ed's heads snap to the voice. A seasoned one. Experienced. Seen it all kind of tone. Face shows it, too. Might've never seen a smile in a million years. Might be that old also.

"Yes, sir," Ed says. "Mr. Stinson." He nods. Exits.

"Jerry Stinson, I'm Ken James, CPA Director." Moves toward the desk. Sits at the chair. Elbows on top, hands steepled. "It seems we've got ourselves a problem."

"I agree."

"You do? Good. Makes it easier if we're thinking the same way. Your shenanigans of the past few days have caused quite an uproar. Started innocent enough. We didn't even know if you were an issue."

There it is again. That layer of the onion, peeling away. Pick on a word and use it for his own will. Do with it what he wants.

"I might be the whole subscription," Jerry says. He tries to resist the smile. The yellow of his teeth won't allow it.

"Excuse me?" the Director says.

"Sorry. Nothing. You were saying?"

Close call, Jerry. Try to keep it together.

"You're aware of the CPA's role?"

"Protecting the world's citizens. Global organization. Funded by, I guess, all the governments of the world. Can't help but wonder how those finances are tracked."

"That's correct. Global organization that, to this point, had done a fairly great job at being discreet. Sure, law enforcement is aware of our presence, but even they don't understand the scope. It's important that we operate that way. It keeps the world at large in the dark. Helps us to be more effective when we need to act."

"I suppose that makes sense."

"But now you've eradicated nearly all of that in one fell swoop with what you did today. Exposed us because we needed to act so swiftly on a well-publicized event. Now, we'll find a way around it, Stinson. We've got protocols in place for that."

"Well, that's good to hear. For you, that is. Not sure how much people will love a secret organization controlling things."

"We don't control. We protect. Otherwise, we'd be the CCA."

"I sit corrected."

"Now the bigger issue is these 'hahas' you've found a way to cause. For some, they've been harmless. Others, not so much. We've confirmed it. Hom Crayon. The *Drive at 5* crew. And now, many, many individuals across the tri-state area of today's broadcast. We're still getting reports. Still doing damage control."

A lump forms in Jerry's throat. Big one. Enough to make Adam's apple envious.

"How many?" Jerry asks, afraid of the answer.

"Definitely in the hundreds. And it keeps counting as folks arrive home, see their loved ones on the floor. Or the coffee shops. Someone getting ready for opening. Coffee pot shattered on the floor. Barista lying next to it. Kids waking up for school, TV still blaring, parents in their pajamas on the floor."

Jerry has no words. No ha is coming out now. This is bad. Really bad.

"Fortunately," the Director continues, "we've confiscated all video of the incident. We got watchers shutting down anyone posting the recording online. The major site's algorithms are blocking it nearly instantly. We can't stop it all, of course. But we can stop a lot of it."

Jerry hadn't considered that the recording of the interview could also continue to unleash its destruction without any more of his assistance. Why did he do that interview? How could he have been so stupid?

He thinks of Hom Crayon. Thinks of Detective Adrian.

Remembers what Adrian said about Crayon. Grabs his chin. Stands. Hopeful. The Director leans back. Also stands. Does his best to be at eye level with Jerry.

"What is it?" the Director asks.

"There's something I was told. About Mr. Crayon."

"Go on."

"The medical examiner didn't have a chance to really look at his body. You guys came and took it."

"That's true."

"But right before, the medical examiner claims they saw evidence of life. Breathing specifically. A, I guess, single heartbeat."

Director James stares at Jerry. Just stares. Looks like he bites his inner right cheek. Steeples his hands again. Breathes in deeply. Lets out shallow.

"You familiar with chickens, Stinson?" the Director says.

Jerry's eaten chicken on plenty of occasions. But the one that comes to mind is the one that started this mess. Crossing the road. Where was it going? Job interview? Lunch with a friend? To lay an egg?

"Chickens?" Jerry response.

"Chickens."

"Yeah. I know the basics."

"Farmers know better than anyone. They're processing chickens all the time. Some for their eggs. Others for their meat. You ever see a chicken killed, Stinson."

"No. I haven't."

"Odd thing can happen. Sometimes, people turn them upside down. Stick their heads in a cone. Chop it off at the neck. Bleeds out no issue."

"Kind of gross."

"Is. I agree. Is. But it's what they do. Sometimes, they just place the chicken on a block. Neck spread out. Cleaver raised. Slices down. Head falls off."

"Why are you telling me this?"

"Because sometimes when that head falls off, do you know what the chicken's body does?"

"What?"

"Runs around the field like it's still alive. Still thinking. Still clucking its head off for feed. Strangest sight. Eventually, it stops. But to anyone watching, that chicken's alive and well. Well, besides the fact it doesn't have a head."

Jerry thinks about the chicken crossing the road again. Wonders what the sight of it would have been if it did it without a head. Imagine that. Headless chicken crosses the road. Might have changed the answer to the question Hom Crayon asked him. Jerry might've said, "Well, hmm. I suppose ... I suppose to find its head."

That's a good ha. So good Jerry releases a haha. Lips stay close, flap as the air is forced out and his gut sinks in. A little spittle flies in an arc.

"What?" the Director asks. "Why'd you do that?"

"No reason. Just thought of something haha."

"Well, stop it. You need to get it under control."

"What's your point about the headless chicken?"

"The point is that the medical examiner saw something she never witnessed before. Whatever you inflicted on Crayon, she saw a delayed reaction. A headless chicken running around the yard. That's it. That's all."

Jerry considers this. Walks to the window. Looks outside. The details coming through. But they're smudges. Swipes. Oils. The outside window is a painting. Some light source illuminating it from behind.

"I suppose that makes sense."

"It does make sense, Stinson. Lots of it. Now, let's get to the real issue here. Do you understand the danger when you tell a ha?"

"I think I do."

"I don't think you do. Take a seat."

Jerry sits again. A little kid being schooled. A private being disciplined. A chicken getting its head cut off.

"These people who have been exposed to the ha, in this brief time, are already exhibiting behavior dangerous to society. There seems to be a lack of concern for others if an action elicits a haha reaction."

Jerry considers the phone caller who saw people hahaing at someone who tripped.

"This exposure has changed how they think. How they act. How they view the world, apparently. Do you see how that is dangerous?"

"I think I do."

"I don't think you do. We have the best minds working here at the CPA. They study, analyze, predict. They look for current odd occurrences and determine what could come from them days, weeks, months, and years into the future. They determine what needs to be done to protect the citizens."

"I see."

"But you don't. Because long term, if this way of thinking spreads, the hahas can become a lot more detrimental. No one is safe. Race. Religion. Disability. You name it, it's fuel for a haha. What one person hahas at may be something that hurts another person. Understand what I'm getting at?"

Jerry saw it. But his brain disagreed. He even disagreed. It reminded him of Robert, Jeanine's cat. Fell off a cat tree when asleep. Landed. No harm. She hahaed. Everyone was fine.

"Kind of like what you said on *Drive at 5*," the Director continues, when Jerry doesn't answer. "How do you think dental hygienists would feel hearing you talk about them like they know they're harming people with X-rays? That they're hiding from the harm they're inflicting? Understand?"

Jerry continues, "I'm not blind to the negative impact. What's happened to Hom Crayon and others. So I get it. I understand the danger."

"Good." The Director circles to the desk front. Leans against it. "Because we have a plan in place to stop the frenzy you started. Quarantine it as best as possible. It involves you shutting it all down. Denouncing it. And more importantly, you never again tell another ha to anyone, anywhere, at any time."

Jerry would stop if he could. But his brain forces him. Pushes him. Go outside the evenness. Break through the status quo. Guaranteeing he can stop it would be a lie. Impossible.

"Of course," Jerry says.

He also knows telling the truth could mean never leaving wherever it was where he was located.

"Tomorrow, Stinson. The Ipkiss Theater."

"What about it?"

"You'll be there. An audience will be there. The attention this has grabbed nationally already, all the major news outlets will be there. We're including others from around the world."

"OK. That's impressive. But why do you want me there?"

"You'll be there because you are ending this. We'll call you out on the stage. And there, right then, you'll admit this mistake to the world. You'll confess the danger it means to haha. You will convince these people who have demanded your attention they should not pursue it. The matter will be put to rest. Then you can go about your life as if none of this has happened. Understood?"

Jerry is torn like a sheet of paper. One side says "yes" the other says "no." One side says "burn" and the other says "extinguish." Any number of opposites pass through his brain.

"Let me put it this way," the Director says, "if you don't do this, your life is over Jerry. The CPA will protect the world from you. Understood?"

"Understood." That makes his decision more evident on the matter.

"I hope you do." The Director claps his hands together, "Our agents will take you back to your vehicle in the city. The parking garage."

"You know I left it there?"

The Director smiles. Just smiles as if to say, "Mr. Stinson, it's our business to know everything."

"But what about my friends? They'll wonder where I went."

"Here," the Director points to the green rotary phone. "You can call them. Tell them you went outside to think, took a walk, found a citizen kind enough to take you back to your car."

"A stranger? I wouldn't do that."

"Then tell them it's someone you know."

"But I don't know many people."

"It was someone you met a week ago at the bar. Happened to see you walking on the street."

"But I didn't meet anyone, and I don't go to bars."

"Mr. Stinson," the Director picks up the handset, motions it to Jerry, "Just make the call and tell them. We can't risk them seeing us returning you or more questions will be asked."

Jerry grabs the handset from the Director's hand. Puts a finger to the rotary dial and realizes he's missing the most important part. "I don't know the number to the place where Detective Adrian had us meet."

"No? Well, we do."

The Director grabs the handset. Circles three numbers. Asks for the details, writes them down on a notepad. Hangs up.

"There. That's the number."

Jerry grabs the handset. Finger in the first number. Follows with the remaining six. Three rings.

"Hello," the voice says on the other end. He recognizes Adrian's voice immediately.

"Detective Adrian," Jerry says, eyes glued to the Director, who is intent on making sure Jerry follows the protocol.

132

"Jerry? Jerry, where'd you go? We were worried. Hey everyone, Jerry's on the phone."

"Let me talk to him," Jeanine's voice bleeds through.

"Me, too," Carl also comes through even quieter. "He can't run off like that. Worries me he won't come back. Then who's going to pay the rent?"

"Jerry," it's Jeanine. "Where are you? Are you okay?"

"I'm fine," Jerry says. The Director gives him a nod. "Just had to go think about everything, you know? Took a walk. Got a little ways away. A car comes by. Asks if I'm okay. Well, not the car. The person driving it asks. Says he's going into the city if I need a ride. So I said yes. Wasn't really thinking. Not thinking at all. Figured I have to get my car anyway."

"Oh, Jerry. I know this is hard based on how it looks, but—

"Jeanine," Jerry cuts her off. He's afraid to take the conversation further. After all, he could slip up. Say something the Director doesn't want him to. And they're probably recording the phone call as he speaks. The less Jeanine knows, the better. "I appreciate the concern. Gotta get home. I just need some time alone right now. Time to think."

"I understand."

"Thank you. I called to let you all know I was safe. But I have to go now."

"Well ... okay. Goodbye."

"Goodbye, Jeanine."

And Jerry hangs up the green rotary phone handset.

"That wasn't so difficult," the Director says. "Now, tomorrow, Ipkiss Theater. 4:00 PM. Be there, or we'll make sure you are."

"OK."

The Director picks up the green rotary phone handset again. Dials a number. Then says, "Send Aspen and Newman in here. They can take Mr. Stinson now." Hangs up the phone. "Thank you for your cooperation in this matter, Mr. Stinson. The well-being of the world's citizens is at stake, and this is the best—

The green rotary phone on the Director's desk sounds an alarm. Double-tap ring. Silence a second. Another double-tap. The Director jumps to the other side of his desk. Picks up the phone. Head angled upward. Phone to ear.

"Yes," the Director says. "What? Go to Code 42. All personnel on alert." Hangs up the phone.

"Mr. Stinson, if you'll excuse me, something has come up. Please wait here. Our agents will be back shortly to return you." Walks toward the door. "And remember, Ipkiss Theater. Four o'clock!"

Exits. Door shuts hard.

That was when the annoying sound started. Timed perfectly when the door shut, the alarm rang. Buzzed the entire room. Deafening. Definitely made it difficult to think. Definitely annoying. Definitely, no way Jerry would be able to stay put in the room as long as it sounded. After two minutes, the door swung back open.

Ed and Leslie approached. Leslie with the shroud. Slipped it over Jerry's head.

"Is this still necessary?" Jerry asked.

"Can't have you finding us," Ed said. "Let's go."

Each grabbed an arm. Led Jerry out of the building. Outside. Click of a car door opening. Eased Jerry inside. Door closed. Front doors opened. Snap and pop of another door behind Jerry.

"Unbelievable," Ed said. "Every time I bump that button. They should put it in a better spot."

"You should just be more careful," Leslie said. "At least you don't hit it when you're driving down the road."

Driver's door opened. Trunk door slammed within two seconds. Driver door closed. Engine started. Vehicle pulled forward, taking Jerry back to his car. Back to this entire mess he started. And now, somehow, on a world stage, a mess he had to fix.

11

JERRY'S EYES. OH, Jerry's eyes. Seemed they wanted to tell a ha of their own. It couldn't be. Just couldn't. And yet, as he and Carl arrived at Ipkiss Theater, his eyes showed him an impossible sight. A hallucination, possibly. An overactive imagination desperately trying to steer him toward insanity.

And if his eyes showed him the truth, then it would change everything because Jerry thought he knew what to do, even if his friends encouraged the opposite.

Here's what happened before Jerry's eyes either did or didn't play a trick on him.

Jerry's ride back to his car was uneventful. Forget the turns. Forget the stops. The acceleration. The occasional item bumping around in the vehicle's trunk that seems to groan. The important part is this:

At a point near the end of the trip, Jerry realizes Ed and Leslie hadn't bound his hands. He can remove the shroud whenever he wants. Could have done it on the way there, also.

"Can I take this thing off now?" Jerry asks.

"Sure," Ed says. "We're close enough to our destination you won't know where we were. Leslie, can you take it off?"

"I can do it," Jerry says.

"What?" Ed says. "Oh, my. Forgot about securing your hands."

"We should have done that?" Leslie says.

"Of course. Otherwise, he could have lifted and peeked at where we were. You didn't do that, did you, Jerry?"

Jerry feels stupid. Dumb. An idiot. The entire time, how did he not think about the fact his hands were free?

"No," Jerry says.

"You're a good citizen."

"Thank you."

Jerry removes the shroud. They're in the city. A few turns and stops and gos and yields and they're at the parking garage. Ahead is the WWLD News Building. Some people linger outside. Barricades in front. Signs held high that Jerry is unable to read from the distance.

Wind up the parking garage now to the top floor. Jerry's car. Just as he left it. Backed in. Easy to pull out. No accidents.

Car stops. Ed goes to exit.

"Come on!" he yells as the trunk pops open.

"Gotta be more careful," Leslie says.

Opens Jerry's door. "You can get out now, Mr. Stinson."

Jerry steps out of the vehicle. Sucks in the evening air. Odors of car exhausts fill his lungs, and he chokes a little.

"We'll see you tomorrow," Ed says. Without walking back, he palms the trunk door and slams it shut. Gets back in the car. U-turns. Descends until out of view.

Jerry's vehicle starts without issue, and he heads down the winding garage path. Gets to the payment gate. Realizes on his journey between the TV interview, the CPA facility, and back, he's lost his ticket.

"Full day due," the clerk says.

"Full day?" Jerry questions.

"No ticket. Full day. Cutting you a break."

"Fine."

His wallet has enough cash, fortunately. Pays the bill. Turns right out of the garage to avoid being seen by his fans. Arrives home. Enters the house. Flops on the couch like a boneless chicken. Stares up at the ceiling.

What will he say tomorrow when he denounces the hahas? "I hereby declare that the hahas are a danger. Nobody should haha. People die from hahas. It was a mistake. Like doing drugs. Or jumping off bridges with a rubber band tied to your ankles."

He imagines the CPA convincing governments around the world to outlaw telling a ha. Purchase a haha, three to six months behind bars. Deal a ha to someone, five to ten in the clink. That person dies from the hahas, life without parole. Maybe the death penalty.

"What am I going to do?" Jerry says aloud.

"Jerry," a voice calls from the kitchen.

It's Carl.

"Yeah, it's me."

"We were worried about you. Disappearing like that."

Carl enters the room.

And Emily.

And Jeanine.

Jerry sits up. Sees all three of them. Tries to get his story straight. Does he tell them what happened? Lie some more? He hates the idea of lying some more unless it's in his bed wearing pajamas and sleeping his life away.

"Are you okay, Jerry?" Jeanine asks. She sits next to him. Places a hand on his shoulder. "We expected to see you here based on our conversation. When you weren't, we feared the worst."

"Yeah, Jerry," Carl says. "I thought you left this place all to me. That wouldn't last long."

Jerry is speechless. Without words. His brain has finally decided the best course is a shut mouth.

"Something's up," Emily says. "I can see it on your face. What happened to you?"

"It's … it's. Oh, forget it. I can't lie to any of you. I didn't go for a walk to clear my head, then hitch a ride back to my vehicle and come home."

"You didn't?" Carl asks.

"Didn't, Carl. Didn't. What happened was I stepped out back of Adrian's place. After seeing all those people that my ha probably killed and the reaction everyone had, I had to get away from it. Then, when I was about to come back in, a bag was put over my head. I was escorted to a vehicle."

"CPA?" Emily says.

"CPA."

"I knew it! What'd they want? What'd they do with you?"

"Took me to the Director. Long story short, they want me to stop telling people things that make them haha. They're worried about the people who have died. They think this will get out of control."

"They actually said the people have died?" Jeanine asks.

"Yes."

"Those exact words? The hahas have *killed* people?"

Jerry thinks. Did the Director confirm the people died, or did he allude to it? Did he respond in a way that made Jerry conclude that people have died? He can't remember. Is uncertain.

"I'm ... I'm not sure."

"What about what Detective Adrian told us?"

"The breathing? The heartbeat? The Director explained that easy enough. You know about chickens?"

"Yes. Plenty."

"I don't," Carl says. "Other than they taste good with barbecue sauce. Or when they're fried. Like chicken fingers. Love those."

Something hits Jerry when Carl says "chicken fingers". His brain. It shifts gears. Wants to spew something of a good ha right to everyone's ears. Clog them up with the nonsense. So much.

So.

Much.

But he pushes it back down his throat. Through the stomach. Right to the kidneys. Saves it for later.

"Well, the Director told me about chickens," Jerry says. "Farmer cuts their heads off. Sometimes, they keep running around for a while. Like they're alive. But they aren't."

"How's it know where it's going?" Carl asks.

"Doesn't. Just wanders around the farm for a minute or so until, plop. Dead. Same thing with Hom Crayon. A reflex. Not a sign of life."

"That hardly seems a good explanation," Jeanine says. "Hardly at all. And doesn't confirm that Hom Crayon or the others died. Besides, what about the case of Miracle Mike?"

"Miracle Mike?"

"Oh, I know this one," Emily says.

"What about Miracle Mike?"

"I'll tell you," Jeanine says. "Quite a number of years ago, this farmer went to chop off the head of a chicken named Mike. Cuts the head clean off, but the chicken still walks around like it's alive."

"Like I just said."

"No. Not like you just said. Not like Miracle Mike. Miracle Mike clucked around like a normal chicken. Well, he didn't cluck, I suppose. Lived for eighteen months like that. Owners fed it straight through its exposed esophagus with liquids. Took out mucus buildup with a syringe. The only reason he died was because he started choking on mucus, and they didn't have their syringe. Who knows? He could still be alive today if not for that."

"So you're saying Hom Crayon is that headless chicken. Seemed like he was dead but wasn't."

"Exactly."

"But he had a head," Carl says. "Nobody's feeding him through his esophagus. Digging out any mucus buildup."

"Certainly not," Jeanine says. "The point is if a chicken can get his head cut off and live, then a man can haha his head off and live also."

"Maybe," Jerry says. "But regardless, I have to stop doing it. The

139

risk is too high. Even if no one is dying from it."

"What do you mean?" Emily asks.

"You didn't see it, but on *Drive at 5*, what I said, well, if you were a dental hygienist, you might have been upset. I made them look like they don't care about people. They know X-rays hurt them but act like they're safe."

"Nonsense, Jerry," Jeanine says. Her reprimanding tone takes Jerry by surprise. "Sure, a ha shouldn't be at the expense of another person's well-being. But if a ha can simply celebrate the action or individuality or observation, then what's the problem? We should be able to haha at ourselves and take it in stride. Just like you told me about Robert. Nobody was hurt when he fell from the cat tree. No harm with the haha."

"She's right," Emily says.

"I agree," Carl says with a big smile at Emily. "I may have never hahaed to this point, but as Emily describes it, it's no harm to feel happy."

Jerry stands. Paces the room. Rubs his forehead. The CPA tells him one thing. His friends, even Carl, another. Jeanine uses his own words against him with the Robert situation. What is the course to take? Follow the CPA, keep his life. Work against it, maybe lose it.

"Well, the CPA has given me an ultimatum."

"What's that?" Emily says.

"Tomorrow, they have an event set up at the Ipkiss Theater. Audience in person, around the country, and the world. They want me to denounce the hahas. Tell everyone they are dangerous. Put an end to it all."

"What?" Jeanine asks. "That's ridiculous. They can't tell you what to do like that! Or us even! What if we want to haha?"

"Well, you'll need to do it in secret maybe. I don't know. They've promised my life is over if I disobey the orders. They'll see to it."

"Jerry, you can't do this," Emily says. "They have no right."

"I don't see any other way around it. I just—

"Ha!" Carl calls out. "Hahahaha."

"Carl?"

Carl grabs his stomach. He's hahaing full force. Jeanine, Emily, and Jerry exchange eye glances. Each shrugs their shoulders.

"'Around it,'" Carl says. "I get it. I get that one. Because you have to speak to the world. Hahahaha." Carl's haha subsides into that satisfactory unwinding sigh.

"That wasn't a ha," Jerry says. "Not even close."

"Well, it seemed like one to me. I got that feeling. Happy. Super joy. Like you all said."

"So apparently, I can tell a ha now even when I don't intend to. Carl's got a weird sense of ha. Basically, I can trigger just about anyone into a haha. What a useless superpower."

"Admittedly," Jeanine says, "we don't understand this completely. But the world needs it, Jerry. And if you go out there and do what the CPA wants, then you're holding back from the good you can spread. Some people have to be brave in the face of adversity. They must stand up because they're the only person who can, even if the consequences are dire. Who knows where this will take us if it flourishes?"

"I don't know."

"Well, you have a decision to make." Jeanine stands, looks at Emily. "Emily, let's go. Jerry needs time to think. To come to the right conclusion."

As if some invisible thread of connection exists between the two of them, Emily stands, dons the same irritated look Jeanine has. Softens a bit as she turns to Carl, "I'll call you later, Carl."

"Good. Sounds good," Carl says.

And they leave. Up. Walk. Exit. Gone.

"Guess, I'll let you think, Jerry," Carl says. "But I'll say this, now that I know how a haha feels, it'd be nice if everyone did it occasionally. Might make the world a better place."

"Not if they're dead."

"Agreed."

Carl heads out of the room. Off to bed. A place Jerry wants to go to. Brush teeth. Remove contacts. Pajamas. Sleep.

And now we've come to the point that really opened Jerry's eyes. Made him see things a little differently. A little more positively. Even though he got maybe an hour or two of sleep, he didn't regret it.

He counted the seconds until his alarm sounded at 6:00 AM. Hit it right on the money. Slapped the snooze. Counted off another nine minutes. Exactly when it should, it blared. Shut it off. Twisted off his bed. Feet on the floor. Sat there. Just sat there.

It was the big day. The day he would tell the world about the danger of hahas. A day that would make or break him. How long of a speech should he give? He didn't know. Make it powerful. Keep it simple. He'd never done this before and he wouldn't again.

And he thought about all the things his brain wanted him to say. The little things over the past few days that bounced around inside that he held back. Stuff like the X-rays about the dentist. Could he keep it under control? Did he want to?

Brushed his teeth. Removed contacts. Got dressed. He decided on an outfit he hadn't worn in a while. Blue jeans faded from time. Bright yellow polo. Untucked. Sneakers. He wasn't sure when he bought the clothes. He must've worn them at least once because they didn't have tags. He felt like a new man.

Down the stairs. Scrounge for morsels. Eat. Wasted the day away until he had to drive to Ipkiss Theater. Carl hopped in the car with him. Reached the building. Sidewalks lined with people. Curbs lined with news vans. Reporters with cameramen, microphones in hand. Jerry continued. Onward to a place to park. Stopped at a red light at the corner of the edge of the theater. The light turned green. He didn't move. Didn't budge.

Just sat there. Just stared there. His eyes spotted the something mentioned at the outset.

His eyes must have played tricks on him. It couldn't be real. A hallucination, possibly. An overactive imagination desperately trying to steer him toward insanity.

"Carl, you see that man?" Jerry pointed to the left of the Ipkiss Theater entrance.

"What man? There are a lot of them," Carl responded.

"That one. That one right there. Looks just like a pencil of a man. Looks like a Hom Crayon."

12

IT CAME DOWN to this moment. Jerry never imagined a few short days ago he'd be where he stood. That a crowd would be begging for him to speak. That he would be about to do something that, like Jeanine said from the beginning, could change the world. It took some convincing to get Jerry to this point.

Here's what happened after Jerry arrived at Ipkiss Theater. When his brain said, "Stop accepting this form of life. Forge a new path."

The pencil of the man. The Hom Crayon. Well, might not be him. But it sure looks like him. As Jerry sits at the red light now turned green, horns honking behind him, people yelling out their windows things like "Let's move it, buddy," and "Get movin', pal," and "I'm gonna come over there, rip you from your vehicle and beat you to a pulp if you don't go, friend," Hom Crayon slips through a side door of the Ipkiss Theater, despite the plethora of people and security surrounding the building.

"I guess he looks like a pencil," Carl says.

"Of course he does," Jerry says. "Tall, thin man with that haircut."

"I suppose. I expected more of a guy in a yellow suit and pink hair. Maybe we should get moving, though. You know, so nobody kills us?"

Jerry eases his foot off the accelerator. Moves forward. Turns into the next lot for parking. Turns the key. Engine stops. Exits the car. Peeks his head back into Carl.

"You coming?"

"Nah. I'll wait. Jeanine and Emily will be here. Told Emily I'd wait for her."

"What? I thought they were against this."

"They are. But they're not giving up."

"Suit yourself."

Jerry leaves Carl behind. Heads for Ipkiss Theater. Stands at the corner across the street. Sees that familiar "Red Hand" telling him to stay put. Sees the people across the street. Lots of them. A long line to get into the theater. It amazes Jerry that so many in so short of a time have been moved by the hahas. That single interview on *Drive at 5*. Who knew?

"It's him! It's him!" a woman's voice calls.

"It is! It is!" a man's voice says.

The lined crowd across the street shifts and huddles. People lose their spots. They congregate on the opposite corner. Cars continue moving past the intersection. But then the light yellows. Reds. Cars stop. The "Walking Man" stick figure shines. Shines a bright, glorious path to Jerry!

Jerry steps onto the street but sees the crowd approaching as a herd of bulls. No rhyme or reason other than direct contact with him. "Jerry! Jerry! Make us haha!" and "Can I get your autograph!" and "Watch out, there's a car!"

The crowd halts as the vehicle runs the light, missing them by inches.

What does he do? They'll trample him. Claw at him. Tear his clothes off. That would be embarrassing. Super embarrassing.

He backs up as they pursue further. "Jerry! Jerry! Jerry!" all coming from different people. Young, old, near death's door. Women. Men. He even catches a dog in the mix that barks. Expects to see the chicken coming back for him.

Now, he paralyzes with fear. No idea what to do.

Arms grab him. But too soon. The crowd is still in front of him.

"This way, Mr. Stinson."

It's Ed. Leslie's with him. They shuffle him off in a manner similar to when they put a bag over his head. They walk him toward the crowd. Each with a hand out. Parting the sea. Separate the rabid fans from Jerry's path. The screaming and cheering continue until Jerry is led inside the very door he saw Hom Crayon enter. The door slams behind, and the muffled chirps of the crowd bleed through.

They're in a hallway. Along the walls are different posters. Some showing rock stars. Other announcing upcoming plays. Jerry's feet feel the padding of the carpet, even through his sneakers. A crisscross pattern of beige and maroon covers the floor.

"You okay, Mr. Stinson," Leslie says.

"Yes."

"You see the problems you've caused," Ed says. "Hopefully, you put an end to this today. It's getting way out of control. The Director wants to see you. Verify procedure and stuff. Follow us."

Ed and Leslie lead the way through a door, winding forward through the theater's auditorium area. Light above. Different colors. Alternating in hue. Velvety seating driving upward at an angle so all have a clear view. A balcony on the back wall and two special ones on the left and right. Intricately carved images of flowers and lions along the walls and pillars.

"Wait here a moment," Ed says. He and Leslie meet up with two other similarly dressed individuals. One a man. The other a woman.

Jerry takes a moment to glance around the entire auditorium again. Not far up and on the same side as Jerry, he sees the top of a head, eyeballs peeking over the rim of a chair. The person stands. A pencil of a man. Hom Crayon. For a moment, he stares at Jerry, but then his eyes focus on his right. Catch the CPA agents. He heads for a side door that exits the auditorium.

Jerry, too, checks the agents. They are deep in conversation.

Pay him no mind. Slowly, Jerry backs up. Reaches the door they entered from. Same side of the auditorium as Hom Crayon exited. Pushes slowly. Door clicks open. Slides out like a ninja. Eases the door close.

Now stares down the hallway. Just stares, hoping to find Hom Crayon. Strolls in the direction where Hom would be at the other auditorium exits. Passes a door to his right. Says "MAINTENANCE" on it.

"Psst," a voice says. "Psst. In here."

Eyes peer from a partially open door. Jerry steps over to it. The door opens wider.

"It *is* you," the man, Hom Crayon, says to Jerry, jaw dropped. "You're him. The one who made me so joyous. Happier than I've ever been. Ever."

"You're ... you're alive. You ... you were dead."

Hom waves Jerry into the closet. Shuts the door. Shoulder to shoulder. Shelves on each side. Bleach. Disinfectant. A bucket of stale water, even staler mop soaking inside of it. Odors battling each other for supremacy.

A smile forms on Hom's face. That same smile Jerry saw days ago. A smile that has haunted him to this moment.

"I was never dead. Alive and well, as you can see."

"But you were dead. Completely. I checked your pulse."

"I remember. I couldn't speak."

"Couldn't speak?"

"Yes. Unable to talk. Not sure how to describe it. Relaxed. Very relaxed."

Jeanine was correct. Adrian was correct. The medical examiner was correct. Hom Crayon hadn't died. He was alive. In the flesh. But how?

"How are you alive? What happened to you?"

"They're looking for me. The others said I'd never get out, but I was determined."

"Others?"

"Yes. They came in after me … but … wait, before I tell you. Do it again."

"Do what again?" Jerry tests a cardboard box with his hand. Seems sturdy. Sits down softly.

"Make me feel that way."

"You mean make you haha."

"If that's the way you made me feel, yes. I still don't understand how you did it."

For what feels like the thousandth time, Jerry says, "I can't just do it. It's my brain. It comes up with it. I say it."

"Well, I need more."

"I can't just give you more. If something comes to me, though, I will. How's that?"

"Agreed."

"So what's going on here?" The box under Jerry's bottom gives a little as he rests more of his weight into it.

"Not sure exactly. After I … what'd you call it? Hahaed?"

"Yes."

"After I hahaed, I kind of blacked out. Woke up at that place. They had me isolated. Asked me a bunch of questions. Several of them. Doctors I think. Would come in, take notes. Eventually, they moved me to a larger bunker-type area. Brought in a lot of people early yesterday. I'm not a fan of sharing a bed. Had to get out of there."

"You hear anything about what happened?" Jerry's getting comfortable sitting on the box.

"Just some bits here and there. From what I understand, the reaction I had—the haha—it put me in a—

The box finally gives out under Jerry's full body weight. He sinks in, crushing the edges. Body folds up like a taco. Feet sticking up. Arms pinned inside.

Hom Crayon is at first stunned. Says nothing. But then it

happens. As before, his body shakes. Vibrates. He bends over. Grabs his abdomen. Howls out, "Hahaha. HAHAHA." Sucks in more air. Releases another.

Two problems. The boisterous nature of the haha surely escapes the confines of their hiding spot. And Hom Crayon is on the verge of another complete haha induced coma.

Jerry wiggles in the box. But he's like a trapped fish flopping around a cooler, searching for water.

This causes Hom to howl so loud it'd make a wolf jealous. Over and over.

"Hom! Hom!" Jerry yells. "Get yourself together. Get me out of this thing."

But the haha continues.

"Hom, if you don't stop, they'll find us. You have to control it."

"Ahhh," Hom says. A satisfied sigh. "You're right. You're right. I'm sorry. It's just..." Another brief haha. "You fell so unexpectedly. Then, when you tried getting out and couldn't. It was ... was ... Thank you. Thank you for doing that."

Hom reaches toward Jerry. Grabs his right hand. Jerry's able to bend his legs. Gets his feet flat on the floor. Stands. But the empty box is stuck to Jerry's bottom.

"I have to look away," Hom says. He stifles hahas through a closed mouth. "You're making it worse ... well, better, really."

The box falls off Jerry's bottom like a turd dropping in a toilet. That is if Jerry stood when he performed such an act, which he doesn't.

They both stop moving and talking at the sound of footsteps and voices outside the door. It's quiet. Two people talking, the words unintelligible. The volume increases to a volume nearly next to Jerry's ear. But then it decreases until nothing.

"That was close," Jerry says. "They're probably looking for me. How did you end up here?"

"Yesterday. Escaped the facility where they had me. Came out

149

to the lot. Saw a car there with the trunk open. Figured might as well give it a shot. Hopped in. Door closed almost immediately. Not sure by who. Jostled around in there for a good while. Then we stopped. Trunk popped open again. I was in a parking garage. Jumped out. Found a truck to hide behind. Stayed there maybe an hour. Until the owner of the truck came to leave. Told him my car was towed. He offered me a ride home. We got to talking on the drive. He turns on the radio. News. Starts going on about a man named Jerry Stinson who caused a thing called a haha in people by telling a ha. Big deal at Ipkiss Theater. Reporter was unsure what would happen at the event. I knew it had to be you. So, I showed up here today. Saw CPA and knew they were involved with this somehow."

"They are. They want me to denounce the hahas. They're worried about the consequences. I thought it was death. But that can't be it. It must be more than that."

"You can't do that. Others should experience it. It'll change them. Give them a new outlook. It's amazing, you know? There was a time I'd have simply helped you out of that box when you were stuck. No reaction. But it's changed. I see the world differently. All because that chicken crossed the road, I asked you a question, and you gave me that answer."

"That's what I keep hearing. The good news is you're alive. This entire time, I thought I killed you with those words." *Words, Jerry, words!* Jerry hears Carl say in his head. "And that means I'm also not a mass murderer! I have to assume that everyone else was in a similar state. Appeared dead, but not. Like that chicken, Miracle Mike. Just like Jeanine said."

"Who's Miracle Mike?"

"Long story. Like I said, Mr. Crayon, this is good news. Very good news!"

"Please, call me Hom."

"And you can call me Jerry."

They shake hands as if they just met.

"And what were your kids' names?"

"Don't have any kids."

"Oh, that's right. That's a shame. Especially since you're the world's best dad and all."

That's a ha if Jerry had ever heard one. But Hom obviously didn't think so. Straightest face he'd seen on the guy. So straight he could be dead.

Which he isn't.

"One thing I'll tell you. They want you to denounce these hahas, you can't. You shouldn't. You have a duty. You owe it to the world."

"I can see that now. But the consequences if I don't. The CPA has threatened me. They'll take everything I have. Ruin my life."

The tone shifts. Low. Miserable. The end of the world is nigh and all that stuff. Jerry feels it. He's certain Hom sees it. Jerry wishes he could bring a smile back to his face.

"Think about what you told me, Jerry," Hom says, pitch somber.

"About what?"

"About the chicken. Why it crossed the road."

"What about it?"

"Makes me think of another question. Why did the ha teller tell the ha?"

Jerry has a response. The obvious one. Right in front of his face. No questions asked. It merits only one. Jerry knows it. Hom knows it. The answer isn't a ha. The answer is his duty. The answer is now his being. The answer is for all to know.

"Mr. Stinson!" Ed's voice yells from outside the maintenance closet.

"Quick. Hide," Jerry whispers loudly.

"Where? There's nowhere to go."

"Here." Jerry picks up the box he sat on and fell through.

"Stand there."

Hom obeys. Jerry places the box on Hom's head. He looks like a tall, skinny lamp with a top-heavy shade. Only thing missing is the drawcord.

"You think this will work?" Hom asks.

"Let's hope so."

Jerry opens the door a crack. A sliver. Barely enough for a pupil to see. Then, it opens fully. This hides Hom behind the door from whoever enters.

"Jerry. What are you doing?" It's Ed. Leslie is behind him.

"You … you were talking for a while. And I had to go. Had to go real bad."

"You got a small bladder, Stinson."

"I know. Runs in the family."

"Problem with that," Leslie says. "This isn't a bathroom."

"Well, I realized that when I came in, but it was too late, so…" Jerry motions his head toward the bucket and mop along the far wall.

"Gross," Ed says. "Let's go. The Director wants to talk to you."

Jerry's not sure what to think about the fact that neither Ed nor Leslie asked if he washed his hands or if he needed to wash them before he talked to the Director.

They weave him back to the auditorium. Down the left side of the theater seating. Another door. They enter. Moves to the backstage. Tables with tall rectangular mirrors and big round bulbs along the perimeter. Beyond that, doors with labels above that say "DRESSING ROOM 1", "DRESSING ROOM 2", and so forth.

They approach a small group. Director Ken James is at the center. As Jerry approaches, the crowd disperses.

"Ah, Mr. Stinson. Glad you're here so early."

"Well, the early bird and all," Jerry says.

"I apologize for ending our conversation so abruptly yesterday. We had a slight emergency."

"I hope it was rectified." Jerry knows full well it wasn't after his rendezvous in the maintenance closet.

"It … it's not something I can discuss." The Director nods, puts a foot forward.

Because it wasn't rectified.

"Agents, if I could have a moment with Mr. Stinson."

"Yes, sir," Ed says. Leslie says the same. They both walk away.

"Now, the procedure for this will be quite simple," the Director says. "Best to keep it short. Keep it quick. No questions. I imagine you'll need some form of isolation from the media afterward. The CPA is willing to offer this until all of it is behind us and nobody's thinking about it anymore. For a nominal fee."

"A fee? I lost my job earlier this week. I can't afford a fee. Still paying my own rent, and Carl's no help."

"Who's Carl?"

"My roommate."

"Well, we can discuss that part later if you need it. The important thing is you walk out of here today never telling another ha again."

They stroll toward "DRESSING ROOM 3", enter. Room is triple the size of the maintenance closet he was just in with Hom Crayon. Small sofa to the right. Another one of those lit table mirrors. On the table, a piece of paper.

"This," the Director picks up the paper, "is what you are to say. Lights will go down. Our host will introduce you. You come out. Spotlight on you. All will be watching. Then you say exactly what's on this paper." He hands it to Jerry.

Jerry reviews it. It's a few paragraphs. States his name. Then, goes into reasons hahas are dangerous. Outlines them point by point: Comatose states, ultimately death, lack of sympathetic actions, the destruction of society at large.

Lots of words for a single page.

"I don't think I can remember all of this," Jerry says. And after seeing Hom Crayon alive, he's not sure he can even say it.

"We're aware. This is simply to warm you up. Become familiar with the words. We'll have a teleprompter at the back end of the auditorium giving you everything you need to say."

Jerry continues to skim the sentences. Collapse of culture. Governments. The desire for hahas spreads like a virus, leading to truancy at the workplace, affecting economic stability. World economy tumbles like a block tower.

"This seems a little extreme," Jerry says.

"Not at all, Mr. Stinson. It's exactly right. This thing is dangerous. Our brightest minds have determined it. Global leaders are in agreement. You aren't considering changing your decision, are you?"

"Not at all."

The Director leads him back outside the dressing room. Continues, "This is important, Stinson. Don't mess this up. I think I've made clear the consequence if you do."

"You have."

Across the way, Jerry spots a large machine of some technological prowess. A few screens. Blinking lights. Enough buttons to make a collared shirt jealous. Wires spit out like snakes along the floor, into the wall. Another CPA agent, Jerry assumes, stands next to it.

"What's that thing?" Jerry asks.

"That? Well, that's what controls this entire broadcast. Can't allow the news crews in here in case anything goes wrong. Controls it all. Feeds it to the networks. We have an issue, we can disable the feed immediately. Cut it off from everyone."

"Hmm ... all because of hahas."

"All because of hahas."

"And you're choosing me to do this. Still can't help but wonder why."

"Because you started it Stinson, and the one who starts it has the strongest voice to stop it. Simple as that. Now, I have things to do to ensure this happens without any issues."

Jerry wants to repeat it. That word issues. He just can't help it. He doesn't even think it's his brain anymore. It's an inborn desire to make a statement that brings him a moment of joy.

"Otherwise, you'll have to buy the subscription," Jerry says. "Cheaper that way."

"What's that now?"

"Nothing."

The Director gives Jerry a confused look but then calls a CPA agent over, asks him to guard Jerry's dressing room door, and walks away.

Speech paper in hand, Jerry sits in front of the mirror. Examines himself. Determines if the world at large is ready to see his mug on their televisions.

"My name is Jerry Stinson," Jerry says, half looking at the speech, half looking in the mirror. "Today, I have been asked to provide a public service important to all citizens globally. As you may be aware—

Someone knocks at the dressing room door. Almost instinctively, Jerry expects to hear Carl's voice say, "Jerry, someone's at the door."

Places the speech on the table. Walks to the door. Opens it.

"Jeanine?" Jerry says. "What are you doing here?"

Jeanine charges forward. Emily behind her. Carl behind her. Door left wide open.

"Nice to see you, too, Jerry," Jeanine says. She finds a place on the sofa. Emily joins. Carl stands.

"Sorry. Sorry. I'm glad you're here. How'd they know to let you back here?"

"She has ways," Carl says. "Never seen such a persuasive woman. Amazing watching her work."

"It was simple, Jerry," Jeanine says. "Approached one of the security people outside. Emily and Carl with me. Told them Carl was your roommate. We're here to see you."

"That's all you had to do," Jerry says.

"No. He obviously put up a fuss. So I hit him where it hurts. I could tell he was one of those CPA guys based on what Emily told me."

"No doubt," Emily says. "They all dress the same and act the same. Other than that, they look different."

"I know they don't want the hahas out. I tell him if you don't let us in to see our friend, then we'll make sure everyone knows about hahas. You can't stop us."

"You should've seen the guy, Jerry," Carl says. "You'd think she threatened to kill him and his family and jump back through the ages and kill all his descendants."

"You mean ancestors," Jerry says.

"No. I'm pretty sure I mean descendants."

"Next thing we know," Emily says, "we're being escorted back here. The one CPA agent recognized Carl from when they visited you the other day."

"We insisted on seeing you because Carl told me something when we arrived," Jeanine says. "Something that changes everything."

"What was that?" Jerry asks.

"That you saw Hom Crayon."

Jerry jumps. Remembers the door is wide open for anyone outside to hear. Waits a second. No CPA reaction. No one charges in asking about Hom Crayon. No one questions about a pencil of man.

"I did. One minute." Jerry walks to the door. Closes it. Tries to be casual. Tries to act like nothing's amiss. Tries to keep his cool. Walks back to his friends. "Yes. I did see Hom Crayon. Even spoke to him. It was just like you said, Jeanine. Exactly. He was like Miracle Mike. Appeared dead but wasn't."

"So this does change everything," Jeanine says. "You know what you have to do."

Jerry looks from Jeanine to Carl to Emily. They all know it. If they know it. He knows it.

"I do. But—

"But nothing, Jerry," Emily chimes in. "This is the biggest story in a long time. Maybe ever. You'll go down in the history books. Do you understand that?"

"And Emily will go down as the one who broke the story," Carl says. "She helped expose the entire thing. She can finally be a journalist."

"And what will I be?" Jerry says.

"Whatever you want?" Emily says. "You want a job tracking numbers at the paper, I can get it for you even if they don't have an opening. But really, you could do whatever you want."

"Not if the CPA makes me vanish."

"Jerry," Jeanine says. Her hand graces his. A gentle touch. "I know you're scared. But if you open this up instead of closing it down, good will come from it. I promise."

"You've always been so confident about this, Jeanine. I don't understand why. Even in the face of death, you've been confident. Why?"

"Because if there is one thing I know about people, every single one of them wants to be happy, even if for a moment. A brief period of complete freedom from misery makes it all worth it. That's what a haha does."

"We're supporting you, Jerry," Emily says.

"Yeah," Carl says. "We'll do anything"

Somehow, despite himself, these three people believe in him. Their eyes lift him. Raise him high. Into the air. Nothing can stop him. Tell a ha. Get a haha. As simple as that. Don't overthink it. Enjoy it. Let others enjoy it. So simple. And yet, he's made it so complicated.

"You're right," Jerry says. "You've been right along. I was too scared to admit it or believe it. But the evidence is there. Hom Crayon is alive. Everyone wants joy." He pauses a moment. Thinks. A quick thought. A great one. A fantastic one. "I have an idea."

"What?" Jeanine asks.

"Carl, when I go out there, can you stay backstage?"

"Sure," Carl says.

"Here's what you'll do…"

Jerry proceeds to explain his plan. Bit for bit. Piece by piece. They think it's a fabulous idea. And that bolsters Jerry's confidence more.

And now the time had come. A knock at the door well after the plan was in place. The knocker didn't wait for an answer. Walked right in. "Stinson," the Director said, "we go live in ten minutes. You ready?"

"As I'll ever be," Jerry said. He stood. Gave a reassuring nod to his friends. They returned it.

As they all exited the room, the Director said, "My men told me about your visiting friends. I trust we won't have any trouble?"

"None at all."

"We have special seats for all of you. Front row."

"Us, sir," Carl said. "If you don't mind. I'm really not a fan of crowds, being agoraphobic and all."

"Agoraphobic?"

"Yes. A fear of crowds. They close on you. All sides. Bumping. Suffocation." Carl grabs his chest, breathes heavily. "Even talking about it is giving me anxiety."

"You're point."

"If I can view the event from here. Backstage. Would that be acceptable?"

"Well…" The director hesitated. Eyes looked upward. Head wiggled a shake. "I suppose there's no harm."

"And me, too," Emily said.

"You're also agoraphobic?"

"No, just … he's my boyfriend. Wouldn't want to leave him alone."

"Very well. And you ma'am." The Director nods toward Jeanine.

"I'll be fine out front."

"Then it's settled. Follow me, Stinson. Ma'am, our agent here will escort you to your seat."

Jeanine smiled at Jerry as she walked away. That soft caress. The warming sensation in his chest. Something was there. She approved. And that approval meant the world to him.

Jerry followed the Director to the side stage. Behind a curtain. The Director went on about the procedure for the event. While he talked, Jerry pulled the curtain back. A packed crowd. The stage was lit up bright.

"…all that clear, Stinson," the Director said.

It didn't matter if it was clear or not. Jerry had made up his mind. As shaky as his hands and knees felt and as much as his stomach signaled with gurgles and fits, what Jerry had decided to do was perfectly clear.

"Yes, clear," Jerry says.

The lights on the stage dimmed. A single circular spot illuminated. A man passed Jerry. Walked onto the stage. He stepped up to a single microphone. Tuxedo. Black bowtie. The closest thing to a living stick figure of a man Jerry had ever seen. Spotlight on him, he spoke a commanding tone that hushed the restless crowd:

"We welcome all of you today to this special event. One that promises the safety and security of every citizen on this planet, from those here in person to those across the globe viewing this by television."

As the Director said, a teleprompter at the back of the theater flashed up the words to be spoken. The man on stage read them exactly as shown. Didn't look at the audience. Eyes averted upward. He continued:

"It's understood why you are here, and that is to see Jerry Stinson. He has an important message for all of you. One that will ensure you're safety and protection. So without further delay, I present to you Jerry Stinson."

The crowd erupted in applause. The man on stage did the same, backed away from the microphone, eyes on Jerry.

Jerry stood there. Just stood. Feet didn't want to move. Even as he willed them. Even as the claps and cheers rang his ears.

"Go on, Mr. Stinson," the Director said. "It's show time."

The Director gave him a nudge that forced Jerry onto the stage. The spotlight found him immediately. The sea of eyeballs followed it. Spotted Jerry. The volume of the audience turned up another two notches. Maybe three. Why not? Let's say four.

"It'll be fine," Jerry says. "Fine."

Jerry moved step over step. Counted them in his head. One, two, three, four, five, six, seven, and eight. He stood in front of the microphone. Looked upward. Spotlight blinded his eyes. Lowered them. Found the teleprompter in the back. In the front row, saw Jeanine. She clapped, smiled, gave two thumbs up. The joy on her face: priceless. *Bring the joy to others*, Jerry heard in his head. The Director sat next to Jeanine.

Jerry leaned his head toward the audience. Their applause died to a still room. Eyes to the teleprompter. Spoke into the microphone:

"My name is Jerry Stinson."

13

THAT WAS IT. The moment was done. Jerry changed the world for good. No coming back from it. None at all.

Let's discuss what happened when Jerry stepped up to the microphone on stage, spoke into it, and said, "My name is Jerry Stinson."

Before he reads the next sentence from the teleprompter that scrolls the words, the crowd again breaks out into applause. This time, the sound reverberates off the walls, intensifies as the waves bounce around the theater. Finally calms.

The sentence on the teleprompter restarts.

"Today..." Jerry clears his throat. "Today I have been asked to provide..." The words scroll left too quickly. Gone are his next words. "Let's a... let's slow it down, please."

Murmurs lift from the crowd. With the spotlight on him, Jerry can make out the first few rows. The others are a sea of black ink.

"Today, I have been asked to provide a public service important to all citizens globally."

His brain tells him to stop. Don't say these things. Don't ruin everyone's chance at joy. Happiness. A haha! But then his eyes spot the Director. Stern. Stiff. Ready to pounce if something goes wrong.

But nothing is going wrong. Not today. His brain convinces him of that.

"Let me put it this way," Jerry says.

The Director immediately sits forward, brow crinkling with

concern.

Jerry puts a hand out. "It's okay. I've got this."

The Director leans back. Shoulders are still stiff. Jeanine's next to him, hands clasped together as if she's praying that somehow, someway, Jerry follows through and changes the world.

"Earlier this week, my life was just like yours. I knew what I was doing. I'm an accountant, you see."

"*Was* an accountant," a voice says backstage. Carl, of course.

"I stand correct. *Was* an accountant. Any accountants in the house."

A handful of claps. Maybe two.

Then, the first one comes to Jerry. The brain tickle. The ha. An obvious observation.

"Yeah, well, it is a pretty boring job. Just a bunch of numbers and spreadsheets. But at least I can count and say two of you in the audience are just as boring as me."

The audience gets it. Not an out-of-control gets it. But a mild one. Some hahas spread throughout and then die down.

The Director clearly isn't happy with what Jerry said when he hears the reaction. In other words, it didn't make him haha but hopefully something does.

"I had this boss. Real *winner*. And if you're not getting it, by *winner* I mean someone who got his job because he's daddy's son. Doesn't have a clue how to do anything but take in the paychecks. You know that type of person."

Now, there are more claps around the crowd. People agreeing. "Yeah, I know the type." "My boss is just like that." "Definitely know what you mean."

"Fires me," Jerry continues, "because of his incompetence. Can you believe that?"

"No!" the crowd calls back.

"Anyway, I leave. Take my belongings, which include a World's Best Dad coffee mug. Crazy thing is I've got no kids. A shame really. Me being such a great dad and all, you know."

The audience explodes into a fit of hahas. Again, nothing out of control, but enough to shake the house. The Director pulls out a walkie-talkie from his back pocket. Speaks into it. Jerry can only assume he's either putting the agent on notice or giving him the go-ahead to cut the feed. At least Jerry's still on stage.

One of the exit doors to the right opens. It's enough light for Jerry to determine who enters the auditorium. It's a pencil of a man. Hom Crayon.

"So then I'm standing at this intersection, wondering what I'll do with my life. This *Chicken House Foods* truck pulls up. A chicken comes out. Stands at the intersection with me and another guy. The crosswalk lights up so we can cross. You know what the chicken does?"

Jerry grabs the microphone off the stand. Puts it close to his mouth. Deeply speaks into it, "It crosses the road."

The audience hahas. Enjoys the story being weaved. The connections of one ha to another.

"I don't mean it walks in all kinds of directions bobbing its head. It's a straight line. Right across the crosswalk like it knew exactly what to do." Jerry mimics a chicken. Arms act like wings. Head bobs back and forth. Runs right across the stage like that. The audience erupts in more hahas. These ones somewhat uncontrolled. "Maybe it was worried an officer would ticket it for jaywalking."

More hahas. It's a constant rumble now, waves raising and lowering in intensity.

Lowers his voice now. Speaks a question. A thought, "Chickens don't have fingers. So why do they call them chicken fingers? And honestly, how gross does it sound to eat them, now that I think about it?"

There's a wave of hahas. Works its way across the crowd, left to right, top to bottom.

"Anyway, you know what the guy next to me says? He asks, 'Why did the chicken cross the road?' So, I said the most obvious thing that came to mind. 'To get to the other side.'"

More uproarious hahas fill the theater. "Medic. We need a medic." "Over here. Someone's down over here." Jerry knows what that means. It's happening. The Hom Crayon effect. But they'll be fine he tells himself. Everything will be fine.

In the commotion, Jerry misses that the Director has left his seat. He catches Jeanine's arms waving in a cross/uncross pattern. Points to the chair. Not a good thing. Not necessarily a bad thing either. He's probably backstage. Wants to get Jerry off the mic.

Not yet.

"So that's what started all this haha business. My brain decided to say something obvious with some great timing. That man hahaed himself into a coma, basically. He's fine now. Perfectly fine. Can we get a spotlight over on the man standing about three rows back on the right here?"

Another light shines, travels through the audience, illuminates random people. Passes Hom Crayon but snaps back. Hom waves.

"That's him. The first man to ever haha. As you can see, perfectly fine. So there's more to this." Jerry now paces the stage, back and forth as he talks, careful not to trip on the wire trailing the microphone. "Coworker of mine, Jeanine, she saw the whole thing. Then I made her haha. She insisted. I mean, without letup, that what I'd discovered with the haha was a gift. Something the world needed. I thought I had killed Hom Crayon at the time, so I had a hard time believing her. But she was right."

He stares into Jeanine's eyes. She sits there, smiling. He mouths the words "thank you" before proceeding.

"So she sets me up with this aspiring journalist friend. Figures we can get the word out. We eat at this restaurant. Not your typical place. They have weird stuff on the menu. Stuff like kale. Lots of vegan and vegetarian dishes. Called 'Healthy Restaurant'. So you know what I order while I'm there?"

The audience waits for it, place is silent. He has them in his grasp.

"The burger. Full on meat full, fully not vegan and *not* vegetarian burger. And *definitely* not healthy. Surprised it was even on the menu. Thought the waiter was going to pass out."

The crowd rumbles up another round of hahas.

"I swear everyone looks at me like I had a third eye that blinks separately from my main two." Jerry points to his forehead. "Which, by the way, I was wearing my glasses, so maybe it was like I had five eyes." More hahas. "I had forgotten to take my contacts out the night before. You know, if you leave contacts in overnight, it sucks your eyes dry until they're shriveled prunes. Do the research. If that happens, the only recourse is to have an eye transplant done. They use pig eyes. True story. I swear." Jerry lifts his right hand like he's swearing on the Bible to tell the truth, the whole truth, and nothing but the truth. Big smile on his face. Teeth gleam. "Imagine the doctor." Jerry deepens his voice, makes it authoritative. "'The only side-effects from this transplant are that you'll get excited when you see the sight of mud and everything in your path will look like food. Other than that. No problems. Not even any oinking.'"

The crowd likes this ridiculous and obvious exaggeration. They haha some. Jerry allows a moment of silence to settle in and says, "Where was I?" some hahas, "Oh, right. The not-so-vegan place. I figure I'll order the fries, too. I mean, they got them on the menu, what's the problem? So the order comes out, right? Burger. Fries. I'm feeling a little self-conscious. Like I'm being judged. Well, I wouldn't want to offend anybody, eating with my hands and all. So I make sure to use my fork and knife to eat the fries." The crowd erupts into more hahas. "Hey, I'm not an animal." Jerry gestures like he has handfuls of food and is stuffing it in his mouth.

The audience is howling now. It's uncontrolled. More bodies

drop into the haha coma. Jerry sees EMTs enter. People on stretchers. But nobody seems concerned. Jerry's relentless onslaught of joy has them numb to everything else happening. From Jerry's vantage, no one is immune. It's as if the communal experience of the crowd encourages everyone to haha whether they want to or not.

Once they calm down again, Jerry says, "I've got some good friends who guided me the last few days. Including someone I hadn't thought was my friend. Just a roommate. Just someone to help pay the rent. Well ... he doesn't really help pay the rent too well."

A few hahas.

"My roommate, Carl, knows all kinds of crazy stuff. Loves those game shows. Can answer any one of their questions correctly. Not that I'd believe everything he said. Like, if he told me human intestines were so long they could wrap around the planet two times when stretched out, I'd probably not believe it. I mean think about it. 50,000 miles of intestines inside your body? That's crazy."

Maybe half the auditorium hahas at this. But that's not the end of the bit.

"Because then I'd think." Jerry rubs his chin. "How in the world did those burgers and fries I ate for lunch travel 50,000 miles to their destination in a matter of hours? That's like sonic speeds in my digestive system. Lightspeed bowel movement. Surprised it doesn't rip a hole right through me. Well ... kind of does sometimes when I have a spicy burrito."

There's so much joy in the room. Hahas everywhere. The audience. Jerry sees the CPA agents stationed in different areas of the theater hahaing. It's entirely out of control.

Exactly what Jerry hoped.

Some people look spent. They haven't gone into the haha coma, but they sag in their seats, melt into them.

Jerry spots movement to his right. On the floor, side stage.

Behind the curtain. Two agents. Identifiable easily. Ed and Leslie. But behind them, the Director. Standing. Staring at Jerry. Blank face. The muscles around his jaw, rather than loose and jovial, tight. Holding his face together in a single piece.

This could be the moment. Step out. Grab Jerry. Drag him off to a prison in the middle of winter. Make him live out his life in a cell all alone. No one to tell a ha to except himself. No one to make haha.

He'll keep going until he's told to stop.

"Tell me this!" Jerry points a finger in the air. The crowd hushes. No longer fighting his brain's urge to say the words that cause a haha, he's free. The thoughts flow like a river after a storm. Raging. Flipping. Foaming. He's just being him now. Who he's supposed to be. "Changing topic a little. You know, we have these computers. We send emails. We punch at keys on the keyboard to enter all the information. So why do we all still use rotary phones? You mean to tell me nobody's added two and two together and said, 'Hey, this would work great on a phone. Make it quicker to dial.' No. Instead, we dial the one, *tick*, dial a five, *tick-tick-tick-tick-tick*. And if your friend has one or more nines in his number," Jerry slows his pace, really draws it out, "*tick … tick … tick … tick … tick … tick …* Oh, forget it. I can't count that high. The point is, by the time I'm done dialing his number, I forget why I'm calling."

Throughout the entire explanation of the rotary phone, the crowd hahas, they call out "That's so true." "I've wondered the same thing." "My friend almost died once because it took so long for me to call 9-1-1."

The Director now stands in front of the seizing bodies of Ed and Leslie. Both of them may be headed for the haha coma. He's going to come on stage. Jerry feels it. Knows it.

If he wants to come on stage, let him.

"I'd like now to introduce all of you to the man who made this night possible. The man and organization that saw to it to make sure you all could be as happy as could be. You see, many could worry that hahas were a danger. Once started, how far will people go to make hahas? Will a haha come at the expense of another? Maybe. Wouldn't make it right. But if a haha can celebrate who we are as individuals, what makes us unique, help others to appreciate it, and all to haha about it, even about themselves, then the world can be a better place. As citizens, we'd be satisfied. Happy. The man I'm about to introduce understands all of that. All of it perfectly. As do all those who work under him, as evidenced by what you see around you now.

"So, without further delay, I present to you Director Ken James of the CPA."

Jerry steps back. The Director charges forward. The look on his face still stiff. Rigid. The only man coming out. To take Jerry away? Maybe. But clearly his agents have all succumbed to each ha Jerry told. As the Director charges, and Jerry moves backward ready to step aside from the bull about to hit him, Jerry's feet entwine in the microphone wire.

It happens slowly. Feet tangle. Body unbalanced. Listing port side with no way to stop it. Crashes on the floor. Microphone booms a drumbeat through the theater's speakers. Crowd gasps.

The Director stops. Stares at Jerry. Just stares.

Jerry recovers quickly. Grabs the mic. Stands. Says slowly and with a squeaky voice into the microphone, "I meant to do that."

The crowd erupts into hahas to deafen the ears.

And the Director? The Director's right leg wiggles. Knee bounces in and out. The other joins. The jawbone muscles pulse. Out. In. Out. In. Hands are twitching.

The crowds hahas die down. They watch the Director. Eyes glued. Silence ensues.

The Director's mouth opens wide. The corners of his cheeks turn his mouth into the closed parenthesis fallen on its right side.

"HA!" the Director blurts. It's as if he's trying with all his might to contain himself. "HA-HA-HA-HA!" Now he lets loose. Gives in to the force he can't control. That overwhelms the body in a near non-understandable manner. Each exclaimed haha causes his head to bob forward and back. Haha. Forward. Back. Haha. Forward. Back. Looks like a chicken pecking for seed. He lowers to one knee. The other bent, arms resting on it as he unloads more.

The crowd joins him. The contagious effect of a person who hahas hitting all of them. Even if they don't know why he hahas, they have to do it. It's a force that knows no boundaries. That'll seek out all in its path and make them bend to its will.

The Director continues. Flat on his back. Staring at the ceiling. Full belly pulsating, diaphragm pushing air in and out. He calms. Eyes close. The haha coma takes over him.

"I think someone's had a few too many," Jerry says. "Too many hahas that is."

That gets a subdued haha from the crowd.

EMTs arrive on stage. Put the Director on a stretcher. Take him off the stage.

"I don't think I can top that, folks. You've been a great audience. Thank you all for coming out or tuning in."

Jerry waves the crowd adieu. Goodbye. Au revoir. Auf Wiedersehen. Pick a language, he's saying the same thing. Jeanine's in the front row. Joins the crowd in the cheers and applause.

A chant begins, "Jerry! Jerry! Jerry!"

The cheers and applause continue. Jerry walks off stage. Passes CPA agents with a wobble to their walk. Leaning against walls. Droopy eyes. Across the way, passes the dressing rooms, including his. Heads toward the device the Director had pointed out to him.

Carl stands there, dressed in a black suit. Emily is next to him.

"Everything go as planned?" Jerry asks.

"Of course," Carl says. "Easier even. Once you got started, the guy standing here went into one of those comas. Dragged him to your dressing room easily enough. Put these clothes. Instant CPA agent. Except no card. Gotta work on that. All the others were too entranced by your speech out there to notice. Can't say I completely understand why."

"Well, I can," Emily says. "It was all I could do to help Carl. Had to shut my ears out and ignore you. Sounds like you really had an effect."

"So he never was able to shut down the feed?" Jerry asks.

"Jerry!" Jeanine's voice from behind. He turns. She's running toward him. Wraps her arms around his neck. "You did it, Jerry! Made all those people happy. Used your gift."

"Well, the people here anyway. I was just confirming with Carl that the feed never went down."

"And it didn't," Carl says. "I heard some chatter right after you talked about that mug, but all these guys were too busy hahaing at what you said. Nobody touched the device. Then, I was there for the remainder. Nobody came over."

"I can't thank all of you enough for this. Helping me. Helping me see what I needed to do even when I put up a fuss."

"This changes everything," Emily says. "I can't imagine the impact this has now that it's out there."

"All kinds of options," Jeanine says. "Jerry's only touched the surface. The amount of ways to haha, the variety of ways to experience it, we'll probably be learning them for years to come."

"As will the rest of the world," Jerry says.

"Mr. Stinson!" a voice calls across the way. It's Ed Aspen moving quickly. Leslie Newman behind him. "Glad we found you."

Maybe all is not as good as Jerry imagines. He broke the rules. Now the CPA would take him to the rest of his life. Even so, Jerry considers the punishment worth it if he's changed the world for the better.

Jerry lifts his arms. Wrists out. "Go ahead. Arrest me."

"What?" Ed says. "No. No. That's not happening at all. I just wanted to tell you. After they took the Director into the ambulance, he came to. Insisted on a phone call. They got to the hospital. He grabbed the phone at the front desk. Dialed a number immediately."

"You seem to know a lot about what happened being you weren't there."

"We do. But that's because he called the theater. Asked for me. Told me he came to in the ambulance. That he insisted on a phone call. When they got to the hospital, he said he grabbed the phone at the front desk and dialed a number immediately."

"OK. Makes sense."

"Anyway, he tells me he's changed his mind. Sometimes, even the brightest people can have the dimmest bulb when it comes to new ideas and change. After experiencing the haha, he understood. It all made sense. I can't help but agree with him."

"Me, too," Leslie says.

"What about all the government leaders?" Jerry asks. "You know, the ones that, I guess, fund your little operation?"

"Them?" Ed says. "The Director has a lot of influence. A lot of goodwill. A lot of persuasion ability. He tells them what he thinks, they generally go with it. So he tells them the brightest people can sometimes have the dimmest bulb, they'll believe him."

"Even though it's his people that are dim? Seems it could cause them to lose faith in the CPA."

"Maybe. Maybe not. Why do you care?"

Ed is correct. Why does Jerry care? As long as no one is locking him up for life, giving him meals through a slot in the door, and telling him when he can enjoy some sunshine, he should be as happy as a hahaing crowd.

"So I'm free to go?" Jerry asks. Finally, lowers his arms.

"Free to go," Ed says.

"And all the others you had at your facility there?"

"Well, I think it goes without saying. Of course."

Ed and Leslie bid goodbye and walk away.

"Well this all seems to be getting wrapped up in a nice pretty bow, don't you think?" Carl says.

The other three shrug.

"I suppose," Jerry says.

And that was that. Jeanine grabbed Jerry's hand. Suggested they leave the theater.

Emily grabbed Carl's hand. Said, "Oh, Jerry. Good news. Turns out the paper is hiring for the finance department. Told them about you. They said you can come in for an interview first thing Monday morning."

Jerry considered the option. Is that what he wanted to do with the rest of his life? He'd cracked his brain open like an egg. Seemed like there were a lot of other possibilities out there now. Maybe he could even make a career out of it. Who knows? Like Jeanine said, they'll be finding ways to make the haha for a long time.

The four-person crew worked their way through the backstage section of the theater. Found a door to exit onto the alley. Some in their direction. To the right, empty, street lamp lit sidewalk. They headed right.

A *Chicken House Foods* truck passed them.

14

"MAYBE ... MAYBE IT was done."

The words came so naturally now for Jerry. So easy. Effortless, especially since he no longer resisted the urgings of his brain to form a new path. His life would be good. He'd be okay. He knew that now.

Here's what happened after Jerry and his friends left the theater and the *Chicken House Foods* truck passed them.

The *Chicken House Foods* truck continues for a block. Turns left. Travels out of view. The whole while with chickens clucking and poking their heads through the slots. Uncertain of their fate. Which, of course, in most cases is a platter at the dinner table or the cog in the wheel of an egg-producing factory.

Jerry, Jeanine, Carl, and Emily stroll down the sidewalk past the theater, another block away. The people thin out until it's just normal passersby strolling in the night to a destination. Block by block. Corner by corner.

"Everything seems the same," Carl says. "After what we did."

"Does," Jerry says. "Does."

"Couldn't help but think."

"What's that?" Emily asks.

"Hahas. We keep saying it so much, the words will start to lose all meaning. A 'ha teller' tells a 'ha' that makes people 'haha'. Repetitive. We should come up with other words for it. You know? Synonyms."

"Maybe hommy," Jeanine says. "Name it after that first guy you made haha."

"Maybe," Jerry says. "Doesn't describe it too well, though."

"How about cluckle?" Carl suggests. "Like the chicken that caused the first ha and haha."

"Not bad, Carl. Might work. Still, maybe we should leave that part up to everyone else. Let them determine alternatives."

"I suppose."

On the opposite side, where they walk, a sound reaches them. Undeniable. Something that a week before would be unidentifiable but will now become common.

"Hahaha," a woman's voice sounds.

The four of them turn their heads to it. A man and woman across the street. Elbows locked. Traveling parallel to them. The man is a good three inches shorter than the woman. Baggy clothes. Blond hair parted to the right. The woman, flowing auburn hair, long coat. High-heeled shoes giving her that push taller than the man.

"And then when he said that thing about eating the fries with silverware." The man hahas some. "So good. Just made me feel so good."

Jerry steps behind the other three. Doesn't want to be noticed on the street. Mobbed by a crowd demanding a haha. Sure, it's good to make them feel good. Quite scary to have people coming down on you in a stampede, though.

The woman's head glances around the block as they reach the corner. Eyes find the four of them. Stare. Just stare.

"Hey, it's him," the woman yells.

Apparently, he doesn't hide well enough.

"Who?" the man says.

"Stinson. Jerry Stinson. The ha teller."

"Really? Where?"

"Right there?" She points a single, right-hand index finger in their direction.

174

Jerry tries to shrivel up like a ball. But it's too late. The couple crosses the street. Don't even check for cars. Just mosey right over. Enamored and awestruck looks on their faces.

"Hello," Carl says.

"Hello," the man says.

"Hello," Jeanine says.

"Hello," the woman says.

"Hello," Emily says.

"Hello," Jerry says. "Now that we've got that out of the way…"

"You're Jerry Stinson, right?" the woman says.

"Am."

"Wow," the man says. "I have to say, that was quite a show you put on there. Amazing!"

The man reaches a hand out. Jerry shakes it.

"How do you do it?" the woman asks.

Jerry reckoned he'd be hearing that question for months, if not years to come. At least until others figure out how to do it, and better than him.

"Magic," Jerry says.

"Magic?"

"Sure. Why not."

The man and woman shrug.

"Well, nice meeting you," the man says. "I hope you do another one of those shows soon. We'll be there."

They turn around. Cross the street. Return to the spot on the other side. Continue walking.

"You're gonna need bodyguards or something," Carl says, straightens the cuffs on his black suit. "People coming up to you randomly like that."

"You offering?" Jerry says. "I'll take it off your rent."

"I'll think about it. Not sure if I could commit to working out every day. Big muscles and all for bodyguards."

"You're fine the way you are," Emily says. Hugs Carl's left arm.

They continue walking. Take a left at the corner. Cross the street.

"Kind of doing a roundabout way back to my car," Jerry says. "Where are you guys parked?"

"They went to the next lot over from us," Carl says. "Just beyond."

To their right, a vehicle whines and squeals to a halt. Black rubber streaks on the road. Side door opens. People jump out. If not for the WWLD News logo on the side, Jerry would've wondered if they had come to kidnap him and his friends.

"Mr. Stinson! Mr. Stinson!" a woman with shoulder length blond hair, dark and thick lipstick, and eyeliner to match says. Microphone in hand decorated with the cubed logo for WWLD News. "Can we ask a few questions?"

Behind her, a mustached 20-something in jeans and a t-shirt, black hat with (if it has to be said) the WWLD News logo, large camera on his shoulders. One eye in the viewfinder.

Jerry opens his mouth to speak. Is this his life now?

"Sorry, no questions," Carl says. He steps in front of Jerry. Hand a red palm like a no-walking sign at a crosswalk intersection. "Mr. Stinson has had quite a day. Maybe later."

Carl becomes a wall.

"Please, just one," the reporter says.

The four of them huddle, Carl behind, pushing down the sidewalk.

"Mr. Stinson! Mr. Stinson!"

Jerry looks back as Carl urges them forward. The reporter follows. The kid with the camera doesn't. He says, "I can't run down the street with this thing, Nancy."

But Nancy is too intent on getting her interview. Continues to run forward with the microphone in hand. Pulls it taut with its connection to the camera that is stationary. The resistance causes Nancy the Reporter to be yanked backward and fall to the ground.

Camera Kid is pulled forward, losing his balance. Camera tumbles. Pieces of plastic crack and shatter along the sidewalk.

The four of them look back at the sound to see what happened. They stare. Straight-faced. Jerry partially wants to haha. He feels it from the others, too.

But it's Camera Kid that gives in. Starts it up, a small one. "I tried to tell you," he says. "Here." He reaches a hand toward Nancy.

"Everyone okay?" Jerry asks.

"Fine," Nancy says as she stands. "Maybe another time, Stinson."

"Tell you what. I'll give you your interview. Not today. But I'll be in touch."

"Deal."

They continue toward their parked cars. Nancy and Camera Kid bicker a little. Wonder what the studio will say about the damaged camera. Van drives off. Turns right.

End of block. Jerry has to turn left. "This is my turn," Jerry says. "You coming with me, Carl."

"I think I'll ride with Emily and Jeanine," Carl says. "If that's okay with you, Jeanine?"

"Sure," Jeanine says. "How about we meet at the diner? I'm starving."

"Same," Jerry says. "But tired, too. You guys go. We'll catch up tomorrow."

This is where Jerry's friends leave and the most unusual thing happened. Well, if we're being honest, a lot of unusual, odd occurrences had happened to Jerry for the past few days. All started with losing his job straight through to broadcasting to the world one ha after another.

Jerry headed toward the end of the block. Minded his own business. Kept his head down. Tried not to be noticed. Hard to do when the world's watched him. Hard to do when he's the one responsible for changing it. Also hard to do because he can't see where he's going.

Lifted his head. Continued forward. Promised himself not to swivel his neck if someone called his name. They'll want to hear a ha. Want to haha. Just needed to get to his car. Head home. Brush teeth. Remove contacts. Pajamas. Bed. Sleep.

Almost to the street corner. Just had to cross over, go into the lot. Get into his car.

Another *Chicken House Foods* truck crossed his path. Maybe the same one from earlier. Maybe the original. Right in front of him. That smiling chicken with the thumbs up. Happy for you to stick a fork and knife into him and start shredding, chewing, and chomping. Trailer full of all kinds of hens. A clucking symphony drowned out by the exhaust vibrating its toxic fumes. Truck parked along the curb.

"Hey, you're him," a guy walked up next to Jerry. Stood at the corner of the street. Not a pencil of a man. More like a cool uncle of a man. Sunglasses at night. Ten-day-old stubble. Leather jacket. White t-shirt. Blue jeans. Pompadour.

"Him, who?" Jerry says.

"The haha guy. Watched your thing at the bar down the street. Great time."

"Thanks."

Traffic zipped by. Passed the crosswalk. Step out before the lights changes and the walking stick man shows you his malnourished form—splat!

"Hey, look!" "Jerry! Great show, Jerry!" "Wife loved it!" "Kids loved it!" "My dog loved it!" "Can I have your autograph?"

A crowd gathered around. No Carl to protect him. Just Jerry's simple form. Paper gets shoved in Jerry's face. A pen. "Write it there," a voice said.

Jerry signed his name. Another came. Someone has some book they're reading. Jerry's not even the author but he signed it anyway.

"Keep your ha on, Jerry." "Never stop hahaing, Jerry." "Who the ha knows? Jerry."

The mob, now satisfied, dispersed. Some one way. Some another. Some yet another.

The cool uncle of a man said, "Guess you're famous now. Never met anyone famous." Looked Jerry up and down. "You seem pretty normal, though."

"Am."

"This light's taking forever."

"Is."

And that's when Jerry spotted it. Could it be? Across the way. Other side of the street, opposite Jerry and the cool uncle of a man. Head bobbed. Feet scratched at the concrete. Beak pecked at the same concrete.

A chicken. Looked strikingly similar to Jerry's chicken. Well, not *his* chicken, but the one that started this mess. Stood on the opposite side. Waited. People passed it. Paid it no mind other than, "Hey, look, a chicken." Pointed. Kept walking.

All the traffic screeched dead. Front end of cars inches from the crosswalk. Red-lit palm switches over. Signals to walk. The cool uncle of a man stepped onto the crosswalk. Jerry grabbed the man's arm. Pulled him back to the sidewalk.

"Hey, what's the deal, buddy?"

"See that chicken there?" Jerry points.

The cool uncle of a man followed the fingertip. Right along the crosswalk. Strutting toward them, head weaving, path straight and curved all at once, the hen ran across the street. Directly toward them.

Reached them. Hopped onto the curb. Fluttered its wings a spell. Weaved around the few people on the sidewalk. Some whistled, screamed, jumped as the chicken passed them. Traffic moved again.

Jerry stepped back to get a better view. Watched as the chicken headed directly for the *Chicken House Foods* truck parked on the curb. Engine vibrated. Black smoke rose skyward from the exhaust.

The chicken hopped to the back bumper. To one of the slotted areas. Poked a head in. Back out. Back in. Wriggled and writhed. Eased the front wings. With a fit, the truck moved forward, chicken half hanging out the back. Finally, the chicken found its way in as the truck gained speed and made its way down the street.

"Well, that was weird," the cool uncle of a man said.

"Yeah. Was."

"Why do you think the chicken crossed the road and got in that truck?"

Jerry thought for a second. That's all his brain needed. It could say these things now in his sleep. Give that tickle. That spurt of joy. That waggle of happiness.

"Maybe ... maybe it was done."

"Done what?"

"Doing whatever it had to do on the other side."

Jerry waited for it. Anticipated it. The smile. The closed parenthesis fallen on its right side. The uncontrolled reaction that comes next.

But that's not what Jerry got. Instead, the cool uncle of a man said this:

"Huh? I don't get it."

Opposite effect. Jerry was happy to be unprepared because he let out the loudest haha of his life. Bent over. Tried to catch his breath.

"You alright, man?"

Continued to near silence protruding from his mouth. Lifted. Relaxed. Wiped his eyes.

"Yeah ... Yeah. Fine. I'll be fine. You know ... there will always be something in life to haha for."

"I suppose. I guess."

Traffic stopped. Walking man illuminated. Crossed the street.

Reached his car. Got in. Started engine. Exited lot. Drove. Straight. Turned left. Stopped at the store. Bought a coffeemaker. Back in the car. Merged onto the highway. Followed the lines. Exited. Turned left. Left again. Straight. Followed the lights. Right. Home. Turned off the car. Went inside. Placed the coffeemaker on the counter. Hoped Carl got the hint. Upstairs. Brushed teeth. Removed contacts. Pajamas. Bed. Sleep.

But not sleep.

Turned off the alarm. Unplugged it.

Bed. Sleep.

☐

About the Author

Desmond Shepherd is the author of many novels and short stories, including the emotionally gripping tale *Imaginary Me* and the episodic series *The Permanent Man*. He writes for your enjoyment, to stimulate imagination and to provide an escape from your everyday life. He thanks you for reading the fictional journeys he writes.

He resides in an old farmhouse in the Philadelphia suburbs with his wonderful wife and three children.

Also by Desmond Shepherd

Imaginary Me

The Permanent Man – The Complete First Season

Futan Vice: The Trouble on Drabble

Unspoken Stories

Miscorrection: Preludes

Miscorrection: Dimensions

Miscorrection: Times

Fram Gage and The Infinite Ability

Fram Gage and The Three Adversaries

Fram Gage and The Holographic Man

The Legend of Kyd Lumin

Something Is Amiss on Planet Earth